"What Are You

The man couldn't
His steel gray eyes
and without another word he reached out,
grabbed her and marched her to the deck
above.

"All right now, talk! Who are you anyway?"

"My name is Leah. I wanted to get away from
the people I was with; so I thought I'd hitch a
ride. But what happened to the older couple I
saw aboard earlier? Don't *they* own this
yacht?"

Ignoring her questions, he held her against
him.

"Well, Leah. I ought to drop you overboard.
But instead you'll pay a higher price for your
passage than you bargained for."

DIXIE BROWNING
is an accomplished professional artist, but
thoroughly enjoys her second career: writing.
Chance Tomorrow is her third Silhouette Romance.

Dear Reader:

Silhouette Romances is an exciting new publishing venture. We will be presenting the very finest writers of contemporary romantic fiction as well as outstanding new talent in this field. It is our hope that our stories, our heroes and our heroines will give you, the reader, all you want from romantic fiction.

Also, *you* play an important part in our future plans for Silhouette Romances. We welcome any suggestions or comments on our books and I invite you to write to us at the address below.

So, enjoy this book and all the wonderful romances from Silhouette. They're for *you!*

Karen Solem
Editor-in-Chief
Silhouette Books
P.O. Box 769
New York, N.Y. 10019

DIXIE BROWNING
Chance Tomorrow

Silhouette Romance

Published by Silhouette Books New York

America's Publisher of Contemporary Romance

Other Silhouette Romances by Dixie Browning

Unreasonable Summer
Tumbled Wall

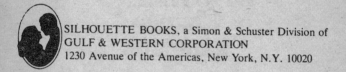

SILHOUETTE BOOKS, a Simon & Schuster Division of
GULF & WESTERN CORPORATION
1230 Avenue of the Americas, New York, N.Y. 10020

Copyright © 1981 by Dixie Browning
Map copyright © 1981 by Tony Farrara

Distributed by Pocket Books

ISBN: 0-671-57053-6

First Silhouette printing January, 1981

10 9 8 7 6 5 4 3 2 1

SILHOUETTE, SILHOUETTE ROMANCE and colophon are
trademarks of Simon & Schuster.

America's Publisher of Contemporary Romance

Printed in the U.S.A.

For Sara

Chapter One

There was really no place on board a forty-foot sloop to stay out of the way, but Leah claimed a four-foot square as her own and remained there, knees drawn up to her chin, while Bryce and Toby went through the business of mooring. She ignored Bryce's mocking glances as he moved nimbly about with bow and stern lines while Toby arranged the fat, plastic fenders. Down below she could hear the others quarreling, with Delia's high, thin voice taking the lead.

There was no escaping, no place to hide and after almost two weeks of cruising restlessly along the Queensland coast, moving ever northward, Leah was about ready to throw her gear out onto the jetty and start walking.

The vastness of Australia had not frightened her, when she had first arrived from the States. But somewhere along the line it had seeped into her consciousness that she was less than a speck of red dust in the great plains and no one really cared whether she existed or not. It gave her a sort of hollow feeling, knowing she had run out of places to go, run out of people to stay with, yet she couldn't quite gather enough nerve to strike out on her own.

It probably would have been better had she stayed in Boston. The notoriety would have faded away and no one would have given a second thought when they heard the name, *Deerfield*.

The *Reef Runner* lurched and scraped the mooringpost and Toby let loose a string of highly original profanity. Seeing him head her way at a trot, another fender in hand, Leah uncurled her tanned legs and stood up. The pins and needles that resulted from her cramped position prevented her from moving fast enough and Toby gave her a none too gentle shove.

"Scram, Leah. If you're going to mope, go below. I've had a belly full of your bloody holier-than-thou airs!"

Leah Deerfield turned away from the open hostility in Toby's sullen face and in doing so, inadvertently caught the eyes of the woman on the next yacht. In the peculiar way of such things, their eyes held almost compulsively while the color slowly rose in Leah's face. There was no sound in the evening stillness to prevent Toby's rude words from being overheard and the older woman had probably been all too aware of the hostile looks both men had been casting her, as well as the slightly inebriated revelry below decks. Not a happy ship, the *Reef Runner*, and Leah was embarrassed for her crewmates.

She broke away from the clear, slightly sympathetic gaze and told herself that it was ridiculous to care what a perfect stranger thought of her. They'd never meet, probably never even see each other again, but all the same, she wished the woman had not heard so clearly what her mates thought of her. Her ego was a limp enough thing without that final touch.

She considered going below. However, Delia and the Jerdins were all in the main cabin, and there would be no place to escape. The drinking had already reached the third stage, with Deke and Pete Jerdin harmonizing badly and Delia giving vent to her poisonous opinion of husbands in general and hers in particular.

No, she'd stay topside as long as she could. They'd be getting ready to head for the nearest pub before long and she might get away with pleading a headache . . . not far from wrong, at that. The only one likely to object to her remaining behind would be Bryce, and Delia would have something to say about that; quite a bit of something.

She could have kicked herself a dozen times a day for having come along in the first place! From her new hideaway beside the lowered jib, Leah's thoughts went inevitably back to Boston even as her eyes followed unseeingly the couple on the next yacht. Her inward visions were halted as she watched the man who had come out to join the woman with the clear blue eyes. They were both about forty or more, settled, secure with each other and the rest of the world, obviously respectable, safe, and stable. Respectable, safe, and stable; these words seemed to ring in her ears and she was totally unaware of the look of longing that came over her thin face.

A little over three years ago she had been at St. Genevieve's. In the uniform of blazer, breton, and brogans, the pleated skirt swinging just below her knees, she had looked scarcely twelve instead of the seventeen she actually was, but she had been happy in a negative sort of way. At least as happy as one can be when one grows up being shunted from school to summer camp to school again, with occasional visits with classmates. . . . But then, she had never known anything else.

Leah's mother had been in poor health since her only child was born, so it seemed practical for Leah to go off to boarding school at an age when most children would have been starting the primary grades. She scarcely remembered when her mother had died, so little an impact did the event have on her own life. Of her father, she saw almost nothing. Her abiding impression of him was of stark white hair, stiffly starched collars and *The Wall Street Journal* in hand. He always looked so uncomfortable and she had felt sorry for him because she had never seen him in anything more casual than a dark blue three piece suit. She was somehow aware that he spent a small fortune having his clothes custom tailored, his shirts hand-sewn and his shoes bench-made, and it always seemed silly to her that he didn't have his shirts made so that his neck wouldn't get chaffed, but then what did a mere schoolgirl know of one of New York's most prominent financial wizards? She hadn't even known the color of his eyes.

Justin Deerfield had remarried a widow from Australia when Leah was fourteen. She had liked Katherine. There was something comfortable about the easygoing blond with the intriguing accent, nor did Katherine seem to mind having a shy adolescent stepdaughter. She had a daughter of her own, she confessed on one of Leah's rare visits home, but as that daughter, Delia, was all set to reel in her man and couldn't take the chance of his getting off the hook, the meeting between the step-sisters would have to wait.

The marriage between Katherine and Justin had lasted three years and then, with no explanation, Katherine had packed her bags and gone back to Brisbane. Leah had had a couple of letters from her; one when she graduated from Saint Genevieve's and another, soon afterward, when Justin had a fatal heart attack. Katherine had been notified as a matter of course, for the divorce proceedings were incomplete at the time.

Suddenly, Leah had found herself out of school, out of family and, shockingly enough,

out of money except for a tiny annuity. All that
had seemed unimportant, however, in light of
the revelation that had he not died when he did,
Justin Deerfield would have found himself in
prison for a stock swindle of gigantic proportions.

Leah had moved into the condominium with
her father's lawyer, John MacIntire, and his
wife, Evelyn. They had been her father's
closest friends for many years, although there
had been a certain amount of constraint
between the two men shortly before Justin's
heart attack.

That had been the first place. Evelyn MacIntire had been a model hostess; gracious, polite,
and reserved. She had drawn her own natural
hauteur about her whenever Leah tried to discuss her father and it had not been until five
months after the posthumous scandal that Leah
had overheard a conversation that sent her
packing, her pride in shreds. It seemed that
Evelyn had not wanted her in the first place and
she deeply resented an able-bodied young
woman who had always had the best of everything moving in on them as if they were a
welfare home.

She had then gone to a great aunt on her
mother's side and that, too, had ended when she
found herself invited to leave and make room for
someone who could pay their way. Leah had
made a stab at finding employment but un-
trained and inexperienced at a time when jobs
were at a premium, she had not fared well and
when Aunt Harriet had had an opportunity to

rent the small room Leah used, there had been no attempt to disguise her feelings about the matter. Harriet Simms had never cared for Justin Deerfield, anyway. She had always thought her niece had married beneath her and now she had seen her predictions borne out.

It had been when she was packing and had come across Katherine's last note of condolence that Leah had first thought of going to Australia. Katherine had the house all to herself now that Delia had married and perhaps Leah could find work in a new country, where the name Deerfield did not bring a frown to the brow of a perspective employer. There should be all sorts of opportunities in a land as vast as Australia, or so she had told herself on the long flight out.

Well, it's three strikes and you're out, mate. The third try at settling herself had turned out no better than the first two. After greeting her with open amazement, for she had not yet received Leah's letter, Katherine had told her she was certainly welcome to break her trip here in Brisbane for a few days, for there were a good many questions she wanted to ask about the Deerfield estate.

Leah had thought fleetingly of moving into a hotel from the first but it was no good. The flight out had eaten into the kitty at an alarming rate and she simply had to make the rest of her funds last until she found work.

It had taken Katherine very little time to assure herself that there was no hope of anything from the Justin Deerfield estate and after a week, she had urged Leah to accompany Delia, and Bryce, her husband, on a leisurely cruise through the islands to the north. Leah had had very little choice and indeed, it sounded a pleasant prospect; there would be six, including herself, on a sloop of some forty feet and they'd make Frazier Island and possibly continue on up to Fitzroy Reef and points north.

So here she was. She had planned to leave behind her three large suitcases and carry only the small flight bag but Katherine had been embarrassingly insistent that she take them all.

That had been her first offense; appearing at the docks with three large bags and hand luggage for a trip on a forty foot sloop with five other people. The second offense had been that she was not willing to join the others in what they considered a suitable way of throwing off the bonds of civilization.

"Come on, mate, pub's open!" That had been the cry that had awakened her that first morning in the cramped corner where she had been given deck space for the borrowed sleeping bag. The beer had flowed freely all day and stronger spirits after the sun had crossed the yardarm, figuratively speaking. Only the fact that they were at anchor almost as much as they were under sail had saved them from piling up on a coral reef, Leah supposed, although both Bryce and Toby were supposed to be experienced sailors.

Her traveling companions included the Jerdins, two brothers in their middle twenties who were taking a break from their father's cattle station somewhere in western Queensland. They were always ready to lead the pack when it came to drinking as well as sampling several other forms of recreation that Leah preferred to know nothing about.

Toby Harris was the skipper, a man of about forty with a sullen look who had made a fair play for her as soon as she had come aboard. He had not taken it at all well when she objected to the accommodation he had planned for her but she stuck to her guns, using the sleeping bag Deke Jerdin had lent her and settling her things in a corner of the main cabin that was protected slightly by a bank of lockers. Bryce and Delia had shared the small aft cabin and the Jerdins bunked down in the most comfortable space, for they were footing the expenses as far as Leah could determine.

It was when Bryce Spivy had made a pass at her under his wife's jaded eye that Leah knew she would have to leave the sloop the first chance she got. Only where? There was nothing for her on Frazier Island, certainly, and she saw little more chance of making her own way in either Maryboro or Bundaberg.

She had decided to try and stick it out as far as Gladstone, or even Rockhampton. The further away she was from the *Reef Runner*'s home port of Brisbane, the better she'd like it. The sticking had been rough, though, for if there was one thing guaranteed to rile a group of serious drinkers it was someone who abstained. Leah had never had more than the occasional glass of sherry, and as her father's brand was exceed-

ingly dry, she had seldom even finished that.
Now, whatever drinking, smoking, and rowdi-
ness went on, she held herself aloof, growing
daily more unpopular until she wondered why
they didn't simply go off and leave her on one of
the countless uninhabited islands. There were
times when she thought it might even be pref-
erable to the nightly bashes after they dropped
anchor.

Leah was startled out of her reverie when the
woman on the next yacht stood up to allow her
husband to put her white jacket over her shoulders. She watched as they stepped up on the
jetty, carrying a bag of what was probably
laundry, and made their way ashore. The
yacht—she couldn't see the name from where
she sat—looked to be the sort with every convenience but it evidently lacked a washer, so while
they had dinner ashore, their clothes would be
tumbling in a laundry somewhere.

Being brought back to the present reminded
her that it was growing cool and her clothes
were below. Maybe the others would come up
before too long and go ashore, leaving her to
rummage for herself in the tiny galley and
watch the lights of Rockhampton glittering out
over the water. Tomorrow, she'd slip ashore and
see what her chances of finding work were for
there appeared to be a certain amount of indus-
try as well as the usual tourists' accommoda-
tions.

In the end, she went along with the rest of
them. At the wrangle that broke out when first

Toby and then Bryce sarcastically offered to remain behind with her, she quietly gathered up her purse and a pullover to cover her T-shirt and went along with the others.

Delia, of course, had dressed for the evening in a handkerchief hemmed sundress that advertised the fact that she wore little or nothing under it. Delia could get away with it, with her flaming red hair and turquoise eyes; Leah would have looked ludicrous in anything half so sophisticated. In jeans and a boxy sweater she had no figure at all, which suited her fine under the circumstances. Yet, when the sun shone down relentlessly, and the others were in as little as the law allowed, she'd peel off her jeans and don the modest bathing suit she had bought in Brisbane. It was obvious to anyone with half an eye, then, that there was nothing at all missing on her five foot five frame, delicate though those attributes may be.

As they walked along, Toby Harris, who hailed originally from Sydney, claimed to be thoroughly put out by the fact that Brisbane rolled up the streets at ten each night, and he was not expecting much more, if as much, in Rockhampton. As a rule, the crew made their own party after a brief foray ashore for restocking. "Tuckering up," Toby called it, although much of the tucker was in liquid form. They had been invited to leave more than one port along the way, to Leah's mortification, when their merrymaking got out of hand.

Squeezing into a booth between the two Jerdins, Leah held out little hope that tonight would be much different. She stared down at the surface of the table, the fresh varnish covering years of initials and crudely carved expressions of inebriated philosophy. Bryce ordered beer all around and, as usual, Leah suffered their derision while she changed her own order to shandy.

Pete and Deke were teasing her, pretending to quarrel over her favors although both men had been more or less decent to her after discovering she didn't play games. Leah lifted Deke's arm from her shoulders and leaned forward, staring around as if vitally interested in the very ordinary decor of the seafood restaurant–cum pub.

Her glance became riveted on the same couple she had seen earlier on the neighboring sloop. They were just entering the room and she averted her head, miserably hoping they would not notice the crew of the *Reef Runner*. She saw only two pairs of legs in matching blue seersucker trousers followed by another in khaki and she heard the woman saying something about getting an early start in the morning and making landfall by night.

They were leaving, then. It was almost as if they were taking with them any last hope of safety and security and that was strange, for Leah had never even so much as spoken to them, nor would she care to call attention to herself in her present circumstances. It was just that they reminded her vaguely of her roommate Iris's parents, who had been so very kind to her on the few visits she had made to their summer place at Bar Harbor.

As Leah sipped her shandy and wished she

could somehow disassociate herself from her increasingly boisterous companions, she cast oblique glances at the couple from the yacht. They were with the khaki-clad man who had followed them into the pub, but as luck would have it, it was he who had his back to her, leaving both the man and the woman with a clear view of Leah and the others. The woman now looked openly disapproving, and Leah could see contempt in the stern set of those broad, khaki-clad shoulders as they waited for their order to be filled.

There was a burst of laughter from the men at the table and Leah tried to make herself smaller as the proprietor glared at them. When Toby launched into a story he told at least once every day or so, one that always brought the color flooding to Leah's face, she excused herself and hurried to the ladies room. She had to pass the table where the three she had been so aware of were seated and she was so determined to avoid seeing them she looked pointedly in the other direction. Unfortunately the man in khaki had tipped his chair back and she ran smack into it. She muttered an agonized apology and made her getaway, but not before she had been treated to a withering blast of disdain from a pair of eyes that could have been chiseled from any glacier in the South Pole.

The ladies room was empty and she stayed as long as she could, cooling her face with a splash of cold water, but finally she was forced to emerge. It wouldn't be unlike them to leave and stick her with the check if it occurred to them.

She emerged from her sanctuary in time to see the proprietor making his way grimly toward the noisy table, and a feeling of dread washed over her. Not again! One of these days they were going to start trouble with the wrong establishment and the whole group would end up in the cooler! Well, she had had it. Let them think she had fallen overboard, she couldn't care less, but never again would she put herself in the position of being tarred with the same brush as that crew!

While every eye in the establishment was riveted on the doings at table number seven, she sidled out of the lounge and made her way to a back door, where she let herself out into the welcome coolness of the night. For once, she was glad of her appearance; eminently overlookable, as one of her classmates had said.

It was only a short distance to the harbor but even so, by the time she had reached the *Reef Runner*, Leah knew exactly what she was going to do. It took her less than five minutes to lug her things up on deck because most of them had never been unpacked. She had lived in jeans and bathing suit since boarding in Brisbane and now all she had to do was stuff her few toilet articles into the flight bag. She left her sleeping bag where it was and hoped no one would notice her absence until they were under way tomorrow.

Not that they would care, for she was certainly a drag on the party, and had been from the very first. If she didn't soon find herself a bit of gainful employment, she'd begin to think her-

self a Pariah! Well, darn Delia and her supercil-
ious remarks, darn Bryce and Toby with their
leers and the Jerdins too! She'd be better off
taking her chances with the sharks than with
that school of barracudas.

She searched carefully for any sign of life on
the yacht beside her and seeing none, lowered
her heavy suitcases onto the deck, jumping
lightly after them with her hand luggage. Now if
only they had trusted the vigilance of the dock
guard and left the cabin unlocked she'd have a
chance!

Within ten minutes she had secured her bags
and herself in an obviously unused forward
cabin. It was small and the bunk was unmade
but beggars couldn't be choosers. Sidestepping
the accumulation of boxes that were stored
there, she reached the porthole and opened it,
allowing a drift of fresh air to enter the stale
atmosphere. If she surmised correctly, her un-
witting host and hostess would have a drink or
two with their guest after dinner, pick up the
laundry and stroll back in a leisurely manner
. . . probably discussing the disgraceful behavior of the crew from the *Reef Runner*.

She busied herself while lying on the bunk in
trying to figure out the range of a day's travel.
She knew very little about boats and had no idea
what one of this class could do. It would be nice
if they ended up in Townsville, for in a city of
that size, she'd be sure to find work. Though it
would be ironic if instead she found herself back
in Brisbane. It had taken the *Reef Runner* over
a week to make the run but they had been under

sail, stopping every few hours for one reason or another and laying over several times when both Bryce and Toby had heads too big to lift off their pillows.

The sucking sounds of water beneath the fiberglass hull lulled her into a troubled sleep after awhile and she only roused once during the night when the boat lurched, as if someone had jumped silently aboard.

The next time she awakened it was to feel the clear, hot sunshine pouring in on her and this time she knew what it was that had aroused her; the sound of a loud splash, as if someone or something had fallen overboard!

Quietly, she stepped over the junk and peered out the porthole, taking care to keep far enough back so as not to be observed. It wouldn't be too funny to find herself staring into another porthole, face to face with Bryce or Delia.

She needn't have worried; there was no sign of the ferro-cement sloop, no sign of the harbor nor the buildings beyond. There was not a single fishing cruiser, no cats or trimarans and none of the colorful collection of cherubs and paper tigers that had been moored about the harbor! Instead, there was empty sea, the water, an almost blindingly brilliant color, and a smattering of blue blurs on the horizon that might be the Fitzroy Reef Islands or then again, might be the Cumberlands, depending on how long and in which direction they had been traveling.

Sounds of splashing came from directly beneath her porthole and instinctively she drew back. Her host and hostess were obviously taking time out for a swim, or perhaps they were exploring a coral reef she couldn't see from where she was. She took advantage of their being overboard to visit the head and there she looked longingly at the shower. It would be marvelous to rinse off, and there was another, larger bathroom attached to the main cabin.

Still, she'd better spend her few minutes reprieve raiding the galley. They had never reached the point of ordering dinner last night and her stomach was beginning to protest.

She was in luck. They had evidently replenished the larder in Rockhampton and there was a variety of fruits and vegetables, enough for a siege. She helped herself to several pieces of the fruit and a self-opening tin of sausages. She would have loved some coffee or tea but that was asking too much, so she settled for a drink of water from the fresh supply in the carboy.

Once back in her cabin she enjoyed her feast and then, wondering how long they were going to remain anchored, she crossed the cabin to peer once more through the porthole.

There he went, arms flashing like teakwood blades through the crystalline water. The first thing she noticed about the man was a bit embarrassing; unless she was very much mistaken, her mentor wore nothing except for a thorough suntan, surprising for someone she would have dubbed ultraconservative. Great Scott, she hadn't jumped out of the frying pan into the fire, had she? She had heard a few tales about swinging couples, but she could have sworn her two weren't like that.

The second thing she noticed was his hair. Surely the fact that it was wet wouldn't darken it to such an extent. The light could play some odd tricks but there was no way that thinning gray hair could be made to resemble thick, sunburned black hair.

With a sinking feeling, Leah dropped down onto the bunk and stared dully ahead at the blank wall. The food she had just gobbled down rested uneasily on her stomach and the feeling was compounded by the gentle motion of the Pacific Ocean.

Chapter Two

How long she sat there on the narrow bunk, her mind skirting the edges of an extremely unpleasant realization, she didn't know. The boat lurched once more, as if someone climbed aboard and within a short time the low vibration of the engines resumed. At least there was a bit more air once they began to move again. After listening carefully for some time, she was reasonably certain there was only one person on board, which meant that as long as they were running she could be safe from discovery, unless boats had the equivalent of an automatic pilot, like aircraft. She wished she had

paid more attention when they were running
under power on the *Reef Runner* but for now,
she'd just have to trust to luck.

After several sweltering minutes, she took the
risk of opening the door to allow for cross
ventilation. There was nothing to do except lie
around on the bunk, alternately dozing and
pondering the uncertainties of the future, and
time soon lost all meaning. Once she peered out
the porthole in time to see a billowing catama-
ran and once she panicked on hearing footsteps
at the other end of the companionway. She only
hoped that whoever it was would not notice her
door ajar . . . she had calculated the risk, noting
that her cabin was at the forward end of the
companionway, with the tiny head fitted neatly
into the very bow, so there was no chance of
seeing it on the way to somewhere else. Besides,
the door was partly shielded by a bulkhead.

Being so far forward might have its advantag-
es but it also had its disadvantages, as she soon
noted when the seas became increasingly choppy. The hull seemed to lift, hover, then smack
the water with a shuddering force while the
engines took on a more serious note, as if
straining to get every degree of power. One look
out the porthole revealed the reason; they were
racing a growing bank of bruised looking clouds
over water that was no longer clear and blue but
a thick, troubled shade of green, laced with
wind-whipped foam.

It was not long before she became uncomfortably aware that she had eaten too well and not
too wisely. What she first took to be apprehen-

sion soon sorted itself out into something quite different and she was deeply regretting the can of sausages, the peach, and two apples. By the time she found it necessary to race for the head, she was too ill to worry about possible discovery; unfortunately, the cramped convenience in the bow met every comber with a bone-shattering eagerness that brought her queaziness to a rapid culmination.

Afterward, she felt slightly better, and with a damned-if-I-do, damned-if-I-don't attitude, she stepped under the minuscule shower and turned on the water full blast, over hair, clothes and all. It restored her more than she had dared hope and afterward she flopped down on the bunk, feeling slightly green but infinitely better, and was soon asleep.

The first thing she became aware of was the coldness. It was still only the first days of autumn here in Queensland and the weather was still breathlessly warm most of the time, but when one goes to bed soaking wet with a stream of air blowing across the bunk, one can expect to cool off rapidly.

The second thing she noticed was a lack of motion . . . a blessed, glorious lack of motion and except for that subtle feeling that told her she was still on water rather than dry land, she might have been back in her third floor room at Great Aunt Harriet's Waterfield, Maine home.

And then she became aware of a third sensation, one she did her best to deny as she lay on the bunk, eyes closed and one leg dangling over the side. She had the strangest feeling she was

being observed, a sort of prickly feeling that
raised the hair on her arms and the back of her
neck and brought about a faint breathless-
ness. Steeling herself not to move, she slit-
ted one eye to peer through a tangle of thick,
golden brown lashes. The other eye popped open
and she stared up with a sickening feeling of
helplessness.

"Would you care to offer a possible explanation?" the man asked, his deep voice matching
in temperature the glacial quality of his gray
eyes. His expression had lost none of the contempt, none of the cold detachment since that
last time she had seen him back in the waterfront pub in Rockhampton, dining with the
owners of this yacht.

"Did you leave them behind?" she blurted out
nervously, wishing only for the more moderate
disapproval of the woman's clear blue eyes.

"A plea of insanity won't help you."

"The woman . . . the older couple who were
on board earlier," she prompted. There was a
note of pleading in her voice that displeased her
intensely, for her pride had taken such a batter-
ing since the stock market scandal that she
had sworn to hold her head up from now on. Un-
consciously, her chin tilted to an imperious
degree, and she gave him back stare for stare.
"I had thought I was taking a ride from someone
else," she informed him loftily, as if she had
inadvertently conferred a privilege on the
wrong person, "but you seem to have barged in
and taken over. You certainly made a mess out
of all my plans! Just who are you, anyhow?"

If she had hit him in the face with a wet mackerel, the man couldn't have looked more nonplussed . . . nor more angry. Like the churning mass of clouds outside, she could almost see the fury building up behind those disconcertingly clear gray eyes, and instinctively she drew her dangling leg up and scuttled to the back of the bunk.

He didn't say a word. He simply reached out a hand and grabbed her, twisting a handful of damp T-shirt up under her chin and practically lifting her to her feet. Then, turning to the door, he frog-marched her down the companionway and up the three steps to the deck outside. She half expected to be thrown to the sharks but instead he planted her in one of the deck chairs with a force that rattled her teeth. "All right now, talk!" he ordered.

"W-what do you want to know?" she managed in a small voice.

"You know darn good and well what I want to know! Who are you and what are you up to?"

"L-Leah. My name is Leah and I . . . I wanted to leave Rockhampton."

The hand tightened on her shirt and he shook her. "Go on!"

"There's nothing else to tell!" Her chin was strained back in an effort to escape contact with that steel-taloned hand but there was no escaping the steel in his eyes; they raked her unmercifully.

"You're from that crew of tramps aboard the sloop that put in last night, aren't you? Don't bother to deny it," he added contemptuously, not giving her time to confirm or not. "What's the matter, did you come back so dead drunk you stumbled aboard the wrong yacht and fell asleep? Well, that's just too bad because your luck's run out!"

"What are you . . . where are you going to . . . to drop me off?" She had a sudden horrifying vision of being put ashore on one of the many deserted islands along the reef with no food, no water, and little chance of escaping.

The man seemed to hesitate, his eyes boring into her very soul, and then his hand dropped away in disgust. "I ought to drop you overboard and let you swim for it," he spat out, "but there are harsh laws against polluting the waters and you're not worth the fine. What are you doing wet, anyway? Did you fall overboard on your way back last night?"

Pride seemed a hollow thing at the moment, and she knew she'd need more than she could scrape up to stand against this man. He seemed to be constructed of iron and flint with about as much human understanding as she'd find in a rogue dingo. "I took a shower," she admitted grudgingly.

"In your clothes?" He looked at her disbelievingly.

"Yes, in my clothes!" she flared at him. "I was seasick, if you must know, and it seemed a good idea at the time! If you begrudge me the fresh water, I'll pay for it!"

"You're right you'll pay for it! You'll find yourself paying a stiffer fare for your passage than you reckoned, you can bet your hide on it!"

They had been headed up into the wind until a stiffer gust came from another direction and threatened to broadside them. Two swift strides took him to the helm and the engine growled as it picked up speed into the teeth of the easterly that was upon them.

Leah shivered and huddled down deeper into the chair, glad of anything that would distract the attention of her unwilling host. From the looks of things, he'd have his hands full for awhile. The rain came suddenly and she shied away from the sting of it, pulling away the hair that stuck to her face, feeling the trickle that followed her already chilled spine.

Misery welled up like an artesian bore as the hopelessness of her situation struck her anew, and physical misery was the least of it at the moment. She'd pay a stiff fare, he had said. The laugh was on him, because despite the fact that she had spent the past week cruising a heavenly vacationland and was now ensconced on a yacht that must have cost the earth, with three cases of expensive clothes, she hadn't enough money to buy herself a meal in a first class restaurant.

Delia had eyed those clothes covetously when they had first met, and had had a few choice comments to make about the man who had paid for them. She hadn't actually said "from ill gotten gains," but it had been implied. It was only natural that Justin should outfit her after she graduated; she had worn school uniforms for so many years she had positively reveled in the raw silks, the linens, and crisp little cottons and she had seen nothing wrong in her father's spending on her a portion of what he'd spent on his own clothes all those years.

So much for a well-rounded wardrobe; all she had worn since she left Brisbane was jeans and T-shirts. By the time she reached civilization again, if she ever did, she'd probably find her clothes either out of season or out of style or both! She'd swap them all for bus fare back to Brisbane, although what she'd do when she got there, she didn't know.

As for clothes, she could wish for a completely dry outfit now, for she was cold and drenched and still the rain kept coming. Her captor was oblivious to it, of course; probably the type who went skinny dipping in January. But of course! She still hadn't quite absorbed the difference in the seasons here. January would be the height of summer. At any rate, he was not the type she could expect consideration from. What was it the freebooters had said? No quarter asked, none given? Well, she might ask, but she'd be willing to bet he wouldn't give, in which case she might as well get off with her pride intact; she had darned little else to keep her afloat these days.

Her small, rounded chin had a tendency to wobble and she clasped it in her hand. It was the cold, not the tears, but all the same, she was determined not to reveal any weakness.

The engines revved down slightly and she glimpsed a dark, rain shrouded mass ahead. She had no idea where they were or where they were going but she wouldn't ask if her life depended on it.

One minute the wind was shrieking, sending white horses galloping across the surface of the sea and the next, they were in a gray-green hiatus, idling slowly alongside a weathered jetty that arched out like a bent nail from a powder-white beach. She could see the shadow of coral patches beneath the surface and from there she looked up to the featureless mass of greenery. She recognized the bunya pine and a few fern trees but most of it was foreign to her.

The man was obviously in familiar territory, for he had idled through the coral heads in a relaxed manner, cutting the engines in time to drift alongside the jetty without so much as a scrape. Quite a contrast to Toby's flamboyant style of handling the *Reef Runner*.

He made fast the yacht efficiently, then without so much as a glance her way, he went below and returned a moment later with a seabag over his shoulder.

Still no word for Leah. She sat huddled in her chair, knees drawn up to her chin, looking far more forlorn than she would have cared to, determined not to be the one to break the silence. If he wanted to leave her there, fine with her! There was plenty of food in the galley, fresh water, a comfortable stateroom and a larger head adjoining it with a tub. Beating around on her own had turned her into an opportunist and she could envision far worse places than this to end up in. At least there was none of the false politeness that covered an unwillingness to have her here. On the whole, she thought she might prefer it this way. Hypocrisy was far worse than open enmity.

Avoiding his glance, she was nevertheless terribly aware of the man. He had shouldered his bag and jumped lightly out onto the jetty and still he gave no sign of even remembering her presence. Then he spoke over his shoulder. "All right, then, come along."

She looked up at that, still unsure he wasn't playing some cruel game with her.

"Get your gear, if you have any," he barked.

She scrambled up and headed for the cabin. She didn't trust him not to disappear and leave her here alone, but when she returned with the first two bags, he was still waiting.

It took her two trips to get them out onto the jetty and still he didn't say a word. She was resigned to having to leave two of them behind in the misting rain to collect later when he swung around and grabbed up the two largest, leaving her to follow along with the overnighter and her flight bag.

The sugar-white beach gave way to an almost indiscernible trail past the twisted roots of a towering pohutakawa. As they crested the slight rise they met the wind again and she paused long enough to look around her. To the right was the open Pacific, its rollers dashing with thunderous force against a headland; to the left, all she could see was dense woods, with ferns and casuarinas almost silvery in the rain. She licked at a trickle of rain that ran down her face and tasted salt, then trotted along behind the figure that was disappearing around a turn in the trail.

Her mind on other things, she almost cannoned into the man who had paused to wait for her.

"Keep up, girl, or I'll leave you to fend for yourself," was all he said before taking off again, the long, khaki-clad legs eating up the distance while she panted along behind him.

The house was a total surprise. She supposed if she had thought about it she would have expected a crude structure of some sort, but here was a strikingly attractive building, sprawling along the natural contours of the earth in a way designed to enhance both. Built of kauri planks with wide, screened porches on two sides, it was beautifully landscaped with a variety of exotic shrubs and vines and she recognized oleander and bougainvillea, hibiscus and lantana, and from somewhere she caught the fragrance of gardenias and ginger lilies.

"Have you taken root? Get in out of the rain!"

Dutifully, she followed him inside, looking curiously about her at polished floors and casually elegant furnishings that equated comfort with good taste.

"Through there," he pointed, dropping the bags in a heap on the floor. "Get into something dry and get on out to the kitchen. I'll have the generator cranked up in a jiffy."

"Through there" turned out to be a bedroom, not overly large, but beautifully furnished with gleaming blackwood furniture and several native paintings of the northern jungles.

Wearily, she slung the smallest bag onto a luggage rack and opened it. Dry jeans, underwear and a boxy pullover would feel wonderful! She opened a closet door before she located the door to a bath, which, it seemed, she had to herself. She toweled off, rubbing the sad tendrils of her leaf-brown hair briskly, before changing into dry clothes.

On her way out of the room, she caught sight of herself in the dresser mirror. She seemed to have shrunk! Never large, her slender five-feet-five-inch frame looked lost in the peach colored sweater. Perhaps it was the pinched look of her face, or the shadows which appeared under her large, hazel eyes after she caught a chill. Not a very impressive sight, but then, it didn't matter much what she looked like as long as she could persuade the man to take her back to civilization at his earliest convenience. Meanwhile, she'd better practice her "yes sir, thank you, sir."

The large living room was empty and she hesitated for a minute, appreciating the deft touches that made it distinctive, before turning away to find the kitchen. Just her luck to be confronted with one of those black iron monstrosities and a slab of raw meat and be told to hop to it!

The kitchen was reassuringly modern, not that she was all that familiar with the best of them. She opened the large gas refrigerator and peered inside. She could scramble eggs and make coffee and tea, but outside of that, her culinary skills were quickly exhausted. St. Genevieve's had catered to girls who were accustomed to holding the reins, not doing the trotting, and neither Mrs. MacIntire nor Great Aunt Harriet had been the sort to suffer an apprentice in their kitchens. As for Katherine, she would have been only too glad to have someone take over all the household duties, but after three disastrous flops, she had ordered Leah out into the garden to pull weeds.

That, too, had been a flop, but now was not the time to dwell on past failures; time now to prove her worth, to show him she could swing her weight, given half a chance.

By the time he came out to investigate, Leah had a creditable meal ready and she watched anxiously as he tasted the first bite of eggs. She had found plenty of them, as well as butter and delicious sharp cheese.

"I didn't know if you wanted coffee or tea, so I made both," she told him. "Shall I open a jar of jam?"

"Sit down. You don't have to wait until I finish before you have your own meal. Tea's fine. We'll have coffee afterward while we lay out a few ground rules."

The eggs needed salt and she passed the shaker over to him but he refused. "The arteries will harden soon enough without giving them any encouragement," he told her with a slight relaxation of his rather austere features.

She studied him from beneath her lashes. He was certainly not paying her any attention, so she felt perfectly safe in sizing him up. About thirty-five or even more, she decided. It was hard to tell with these outdoor types. Not handsome in any classical way but all the same, there was something about those rough hewn features, an air of assurance that spoke volumes. He obviously didn't care a tinker's dam what anyone else thought of him and that in itself cast a pretty powerful spell. It was a hard face and yet there were laughter lines beside the wide mouth and that bottom lip, despite an overall harshness, had a touch of sensuality that struck a faint warning note deep inside her.

"Seen enough?" he asked laconically, causing her to flush and fumble with her napkin.

"I'm sorry," she muttered. "I didn't mean to be rude."

"No problem." He raised those remarkably clear gray eyes and swept her with a glance that missed nothing. "We'll both make a survey so we know just where we stand from the beginning. My name is Smith Cairington and I don't make a habit of picking up hitch-hikers, either ashore or at sea."

Stung by the derision he hardly bothered to hide, she lifted her chin and leveled her gaze at him, striving to make it as cool and as detached as his had been. "My name is Leah Deerfield and I'm not in the habit of hitching rides, either on land or on sea."

"A well met pair, wouldn't you say?" There was an added glint in his eyes but he looked as if a smile would have cracked that granite face wide open.

"If you're finished I'll wash the dishes," she told him, reaching for his plate.

"Leave them for a few minutes. We'll have coffee on the porch."

"I don't . . ." she began.

"I said leave them!"

There was no arguing with that tone of voice; she slapped cups and saucers onto the tray and unplugged the electric kettle. By the time she had located cream and poured it into a pitcher he had already left the room and she followed, praying she wouldn't trip and spill the works. She had eaten practically nothing, her nerves too strained to get a bite past her lips, and now she was trembling at the thought of the coming ordeal. Would he throw her out immediately or wait until morning? Regardless of when it happened, she had no idea where she was, much less where she could go.

"Over there." He indicated a low table between two thickly cushioned chaise longues and she settled the tray down carefully, seating herself on the foot of the chaise to pour. The cup rattled in its saucer as she passed it over.

"Now, Leah Deerfield, will you tell me just what was the idea of stowing away aboard the *Sunfisher*? You couldn't have known I was going to be on board because no one knew except my immediate family. I can only assume that you found out somehow . . . maybe you guessed when you saw us together at the pub last night. So you thought you'd come along and once we were out to sea together, you'd be holding all the aces." His sneer said quite clearly what he thought of this idea. "Far better looking girls than you have tried it and it won't work," he

continued. "I don't flatter myself it hasn't anything to do with my fatal charm, so it can only be
the Cairington empire. If you had some idea of
helping yourself to the honey, you picked the
wrong Cairington." He leaned back and leveled
her with a cool, triumphant stare.

Leah stared back at him look for look for the
simple reason that she couldn't think of a word
to say to his charges. She was utterly at sea, in
more than the figurative sense.

"Well?" he prompted when the silence had
spun out between them like threads of shivering
glass. "Who put you up to this? Mickey? James?
Certainly no one in that crew of deadbeats I saw
you with last night because I'm reasonably
sure . . . just who were they, anyway?" he asked
with suddenly narrowed eyes.

"T-Toby Harris and Bryce and Delia Spivy.
The Jerdins, too . . . Deke and Pete. Do you
know any of them? They never mentioned you,
not that I can remember."

"Jerdins? The Tibooburra Jerdins? That pair
of Ed Jerdins. They've had a hand in every
imaginable scrape since they got out of school
but I don't get the point of a prank like this."

"And I don't get the point of the whole thing,"
she flung at him, nerves suddenly stretched
beyond endurance. "I've never heard of you
or . . . or James and Mickey or anyone else,
much less your empire! Are you some sort of
king, then? Is it to be off with my head? I think
I'd have preferred walking the plank!"

Under the pewter fixture her eyes glittered

dangerously as tears brimmed over and hung precariously from her lashes, and her hands were whitened fists beside her rigid body.

He weighed her silently for an endless moment. There was wariness in the very set of his shoulders and she waited hopelessly for the verdict. Guilty of heaven knows what crime, was she to be thrown summarily out into the dark to make her way through the forest to whatever civilization there was on this benighted island?

"You aren't a friend of my brothers, Mickey or James, then? No one put you up to it? I take it this was all your own idea. Hmmmm." He tilted his head and stroked the square jaw that was beginning to show need of a shave. "I don't suppose you'd care to tell me what prompted you to choose the *Sunfisher* over all the others in the harbor."

"For the last time, I never heard of you, your brothers or anyone else in the royal Cairington family! As for the *Sunfisher*, she could have been the *Titanic* for all I cared! I . . . I simply had to get away, that's all." Her voice dropped to a softer, more bitter note. "You saw them. Can you blame me? As for why I picked this boat, I saw the couple who were on it yesterday and they looked so . . . so kind. So decent. I thought that if I could just get away from the *Reef Runner,* I could go somewhere fresh, start over. They . . . the man and woman I saw looked as if they might be willing to point me in the right direction and send me off with a bon voyage and . . . and . . ." her voice broke and she knew it was time to shut up before she disgraced herself.

He stroked his stubble reflectively for a moment more before he spoke. "They are kind and decent, as a matter of fact. No doubt if the situation had been different, you'd have landed in clover, but you lucked out this time, I'm afraid."

"Will you just tell me one thing? Where are we? Who lives here?"

"That's two things but I'll be generous. We're on Chance Island and I live here . . . at the moment."

"Nobody else?" Her hopes plunged.

"Nobody else . . . at the moment," he told her with a baffling expression. "We're quite alone and unless you want to take your chances in the bush or with the sharks, you'll do as I say with no questions asked . . . understood?"

The porch suddenly seemed vast and gloomy, with shadows closing in around the two of them. Outside a seabird blown off course by the dying easterly screamed irately.

"Understood," she whispered.

Chapter Three

Bludgeoned mercifully into almost immediate sleep by her overwrought emotions, Leah was awakened the next morning by the persistent flute-note of a tui. She made several tries before she was able to sort out the events of the previous day in her mind.

This was getting to be a habit, a bad one, this waking up and having to figure whose bed she was in this time. In this particular case, she might well hope her luck held, for the innerspring was fantastically comfortable, far better than the MacIntire's sofa bed or Aunt Harriet's lumpy pad that always felt damp. As for the borrowed sleeping bag on the cabin floor, there was no comparison!

Feeling a completely illogical sense of well-being, she stretched and climbed out of bed, surveying her stack of luggage. She had not dared unpack the night before . . . tempting fate. Not until she had reached some sort of understanding with Smith Cairington would she so much as place a comb or her brush on the dresser. She'd probably be handed her walking papers soon enough and it would be mortifying if she had already spread herself out so presumptuously. She could well imagine his leathery comments in *that* case!

The kitchen was spotless and not until she stood in the doorway did she remember that she had never got around to washing the dishes last night. After reaching a tentative agreement between them—on her part that she might stay at least the night and on his that she had not deliberately set out to infiltrate his kingdom, whatever *that* was—she had been glad to escape and had barely managed to pull out her nightgown and toothbrush before collapsing into bed, all thoughts of chores dispersed.

Well, either the man had a silent housekeeper or he was pretty self-sufficient. He had admitted to living here alone, but his type wouldn't consider a housekeeper worth mentioning. Kingdom, indeed! It was a wonder he hadn't used the royal We!

The coffee was already made and she helped herself to a cup, savoring its biting bitterness as she poked about in the pantry for something to eat. Cereal or toast would be better than nothing. She thought longingly of the perennial oatmeal at St. Genevieve's and the thought prompted a grin. Never did she think she'd be longing for any aspect of those years of incarceration. She had lived for the holidays, spent with one girl or another at their homes. It had always been a source of embarrassment to her that she was in no position to return their hospitality, but then, Justin could hardly tolerate her own company, much less that of another unfledged schoolgirl.

"Making yourself at home, I see," remarked Smith Cairington from the open doorway that led to the back of the property. He all but filled the opening, blocking the view of lush, tropical greenery.

Caught with her hand in a box of cookies, Leah could only stare guiltily. "H-have you had your breakfast yet?" she asked him finally, though she knew he must have, for the coffee had been made when she came to the kitchen.

"I made do with cheese and toast this morning. From now on, I'd prefer steak and potatoes or steak, eggs and fresh fruit. Coffee for breakfast, beer at midday, tea at evening and wine with dinner, followed by coffee."

Leah swallowed convulsively. That sounded alarmingly like orders to the chef.

"The cleaning gear is in the utility room, off there . . . washer as well. Take advantage of the sunshine while you have it but on rainy days, use the dryer. We'll have plenty of those. I'll be supplying fresh seafood for the most part, but at any rate, there's plenty of food in the freezer. Milk will be canned, I'm afraid, after we run through the batch I brought from the mainland, but that's about the only sacrifice we'll be called on to make. There's a vegetable garden in the back and a few fruit trees. Anything else I haven't covered? Oh, I like my steaks rare."

Stunned, she simply nodded her head.

"Oh, and one other thing. I came here to Chance for privacy. You can go wherever you like when your chores are done, just stay out of my way. If you've any questions, save them for meal times."

Without giving her time to reply, could she have found the words, Smith turned and left the way he had come, leaving Leah standing limply in the middle of the gay red and yellow kitchen, the cookie box dangling from her nerveless fingers.

By eleven o'clock she had made the two beds, unpacked her bags and located that most prized article, a cookbook. By twelve thirty she was surveying dolefully what was to have been lamb cutlets and parsley potatoes. The cutlets resembled the soles of long discarded shoes and the potatoes were stuck to the bottom of the pan and smelled terrible! She had opened both windows as well as the back door and waved the air out with a towel and in desperation, she sprayed the room with her favorite scent, a ridiculously expensive French perfume.

By a quarter of one she was seated at the formica table with a glass of lemonade, pouring over the cookbook again when the door flew open and Smith entered in a cloud of profanity.

"What is going on in here? The place smells like a cheap bordello!"

"Cheap! I'll have you know that's the most expensive scent I'm ever likely to be able to afford again!" she flung at him, slamming the book closed.

"Something's burning!"

"You mean besides your temper?" she asked sweetly.

Three strides took him to the range where he lifted the lids and discovered her mistakes. "Good heavens, how long did it take you to prepare this burnt offering?"

"Long enough." She stood up, the fight drained out of her, and watched while he scraped the mess into the trash and put the pans in to soak. She was hungry, too! Breakfast had been practically nonexistent. "Shall I open a can of soup? There are some potato chips, and I could do a salad."

"How do you expect me to keep anything down in a room that reeks to high heaven? Make it sandwiches and bring it outside. Better make it three for me, and beer." No please, no thank you, he simply left her to put together something decent enough to take away the impression of her first attempt.

So much for my first day on the job, she thought wryly. This was what she had been afraid of whenever she thought of attempting to enter the labor force. Jobs were thin enough on the ground for even the skilled and experienced but for someone whose sole experience had been teaching handicapped children to stay afloat at a summer camp, she hadn't a hope.

Bearing a tray stacked with four thick, untidy sandwiches and a can of beer and a soft drink, she made her way around the house. He might have mentioned where to find him! She passed through the garden, where ginger lilies and canna mingled with New Zealand spinach and root crops, paused in the trellised arbor under the rampant bougainvillea to look down on the iny, blindingly white harbor with its crooked jetty. The *Sunfisher* rode peacefully on the smooth, aquamarine surface of the water, and she suddenly felt hot and tired. She determined to take the first opportunity for a swim, and then moved on around the house, where she finally located Smith Cairington.

He was in a small clearing working on what appeared to be miles of cobwebby monofilament net. With a curt nod, he indicated a place to put down her burden and went on working, attaching a heavier line filled with colorful floats to the body of the seine.

Dropping down onto an upturned wooden box, she bit into her own sandwich and watched the movement of his throat as he tipped his head back for a draught of beer. His faded blue shirt was stained with perspiration and it fell open down the front, revealing a bronzed chest that could only be called brawny. She looked away hastily from the tightly curled dark hair that trailed down to disappear under his silver

buckled belt, recalling all too vividly that the
tan didn't stop at his beltline.

Sandwich poised in midair, Leah suddenly
became aware that he was returning her look,
with a mocking one of his own. She mumbled
something about getting herself another sandwich and fled, hearing his laughter following
her all the way to the back door. Him and his
arrogant conceit! The man knew exactly the
effect he had on women . . . if he even considered her a woman. From the way he had treated
her so far, he looked on her as a kitchen appli-
ance!

Finishing her own lunch in the slightly sickening air of the kitchen, she decided to hold off
planning supper until she knew whether or not
he was going to provide seafood. With fish she
could do the salad . . . at least she wouldn't
burn that . . . and try potatoes again. At the
moment, however, she planned to explore the
island a bit.

Following a narrow bush-track, she skirted
the garden and left the grounds for thick, but
relatively open woods. There in the shade, she
was soon drenched, for every frond, needle and
leaf had saved its burden from last night's
rain to shower her as she walked beneath them.
As if that weren't enough, the fringe of toi-toi
soon drenched her sneakers and the legs of her
jeans flapped disconsolately around her ankles,
as the swaying sea heads brushed against her
face.

The raucous cries of gulls, terns and gannets
seemed to echo hollowly as if from miles away.

Was it possible that the island could be so large?
Could there be a village on it, or at least another
family? Or would she, operating at her usual
peak efficiency, find herself hopelessly lost,
dependent on the condescending Smith Cairington to rescue her?

Breaking into a clearing, her spirits lifted
immediately. The sound of the surf could be
heard quite clearly and she dropped down into a
shallow gully, almost stumbling over a fallen
pandanus, and then climbed a rocky slope to
find herself on the edge of nowhere! Far below
her the sea smashed itself on barrier arms of
coral that encircled a perfect pool about three
hundred feet or so across.

Leah stood enchanted for several minutes as
the fresh breeze whipped her hair across her
face. The hair ribbon that held her long, wavy
brown hair back into a pony tail had long since
caught itself on a supplejack or black cane vine
and now she grabbed the blowing mass in both
hands and held it back while she searched for
the best way down to the pool.

Before descending the more or less clear cut
rocky trail, she took one last look about her from
the vantage point of the cliff. There was no other
soul in sight, no house, no jetty, no boat; only a
dozen or so assorted beach birds and herself,
and before she even reached the tiny half moon
beach, she was unbuttoning her shirt.

Pure paradise, the thought, sweeping the private beach with a beatific smile. She did take
time to spread her wet clothes and her sandy
sneakers out on a rock in the sun, anchoring

them against an errant breeze with small rocks. She stood for half a minute in bra and briefs, and then, with deft, graceful movements, she shucked them as well. Dressing again in damp jeans was bad enough without having to put them on over clammy underwear. Besides, she had a hidden secret curiosity about swimming nude ever since Bryce and Delia had tried to get her to join the others. They hadn't had any compunctions about mixed skinny dipping, but Leah had always found something pressing to occupy her elsewhere whenever they began peeling down to go over the side.

It was heavenly! She had no qualms about swimming alone, for she was a strong swimmer. She had learned at the gym pool at school and perfected the art on summer vacations with Iris and her family. Since she was fourteen, too, there had been the summer camp job, not that it had paid anything except enormous satisfaction.

Thinking back to the thrill of watching children whose lives on dry land were circumscribed by braces, chairs, and crutches discover the thrill of freedom afloat, she wished she could bring them all for a visit to Chance Island. She'd hate to think what Smith Cairington would say to that idea, him with his overweening arrogance and his pathological desire for privacy. Imagine, a whole island for one man alone!

She ducked beneath the water, rolled over in a slow, graceful arc and floated to the surface, spreading her arms wide as she felt the sun beat down on her bare body. She could see

little red squiggles against her closed eyelids
and she made a game of trying to hold them still.
Dimly, with half a mind, she considered the
possibilities of getting away from the island and
from there, went on to consider the even more
remote possibility of finding work. At least here
she had room and board.

She kicked her feet, propelling herself to the
outer rim of the natural pool, then turned to
follow its perimeter until it began to climb into
the cliff from which she had first looked down.
Halfway up the incline was a spreading pohutu-
ka, shedding its fading crimson blossoms so that
they rimmed the rocks and drifted out on the
water. Nature seemed to have spread these
islands over with a lavish hand. She let her eyes
follow the contours of the ridge, its crest sometimes bold against a cerulean sky, sometimes
softened with the tops of trees, and just as the
sun moted her wet, tangled lashes, she glimpsed
something that caused her to flounder and half
sink. She spluttered as the water closed over her
face and blinked to look again, hoping to see a
bare tree or an odd rock formation, but no such
luck. Those broad shoulders, the wide braced
legs, feet firmly planted against the rocky soil,
and the slightly quizzical tilt to the dark head
were unmistakable.

No hope that he hadn't seen her, for as soon as
she began to paddle herself closer to the shadowy protection of the edge, he dropped down
from the ridge and began the easy descent,
scarcely looking where he put his feet. Within
minutes he had passed her clothes, spread out

on the low rocks like colorful signals, and stood
at the edge of the water.

"Shall I join you or are you ready to come
out?" he called.

It was Smith, of course. No matter how many
people had been on the island, she could never
mistake that proud carriage, the wedge-shaped
build. How long had he been standing there?
How much could he see from that distance? She
felt her face growing warm despite the coolness
of the water and she back paddled slowly, never
taking her eyes from where he stood.

"I'm ready to come out, only you'll have to go."

"I'm not ready to go, so you'll have to please
yourself," he answered laconically.

His voice carried clearly over the susurrus of
the surf and it was only then that Leah became
aware of the chill that was beginning to creep up
her limbs. It was late March, after all, and
despite such unbelievably soft days, summer
was almost over.

"Please, can't you go so that I can come out?"

Even from this distance she could see his
shrug, a supple movement of broad shoulders
that was far more expressive than words. Her
embarrassment was nothing at all to him. He
probably didn't even look on her as a woman,
something she had suspected anyway, and she
didn't know whether to be relieved or incensed.
None of which mattered at the moment.

"Turn away then, please!"

Something in her voice evidently reached
him, for he turned and began to walk toward the
other arm of the cliff, leaving her to make her

way to where she had left her clothes. She swam the several yards quickly, wading through the extended shallows, watching him warily all the while. He stopped once to pick up something from the beach and then he turned and tossed it out to sea but he didn't return, nor did he make any more mocking comments.

She reached her clothes and trod on her pantsleg before she realized it, so intent was she on watching the silhouetted figure moving down the beach.

Having no towel, she twisted irritably as she struggled to pull her panties over wet hips. Her jeans were even worse and she stuffed her bra in her pocket, whipped her shirt on and grabbed her shoes in her hand. Without waiting to see whether or not he was headed her way, she started climbing.

He was there before her. Whether he had headed back before she had even finished dressing or his long legs had simply eaten up the distance, Leah's heart sank. Then plummeted further at the expression on his face. Even inexperienced as she was, she had no trouble reading the mockery there, but it was that other factor that puzzled her, something that seemed to hover just beneath the clear surface of those gray eyes that left her feeling hollow inside.

"Put on your shoes," he ordered, his eyes raking her thoroughly then coming back to linger on her breasts, all too well defined beneath the damp, soft cotton shirt.

"They're wet and sandy. I'd rather go bare-footed."

"I'll not have you coming down with a septic foot after stepping on a sharp rock or a thorn. Do I have to put them on for you?"

Thinning her lips ominously, she knelt and slipped on the wet canvas shoes. They felt terrible, what with sand both inside and out and no socks, they'd probably rub a blister on her heel before they were halfway home.

"There! Are you satisfied now?" she demanded, standing up so quickly her head swam. She glared up at him boldly, but wide, slightly nearsighted hazel eyes had none of the force of narrowed, glittering gray ones and her own soon dropped.

"Hardly, but then that's not the issue at stake, is it?"

Some veiled insinuation in his voice brought the color flooding to her face. She would have given anything at that moment to be half a world away, playing double solitaire with Great Aunt Harriet before a skimpy grate. It had been a frigid, barren sort of existence but at least it was safe. Here, she was floundering out of her depth and she had no idea what she could do about it.

His next words stopped her as she turned toward the bush-trail. "While I'm sure your former companions thought nothing of a little playful nudity, I'd prefer it if you'd wear a suit while you're here." Before she could sputter a denial, he continued, his voice as flat as the silver buckle that gleamed on his narrow belt. "And you'll oblige me by not swimming alone. While there's little danger of sharks inside the reef, occasionally a higher than usual tide traps one and I'd prefer to know what's happened if you turn up missing."

"You're hateful!" The words were wrung from her as she stared, aghast up into his graven face. "I think I'd prefer the sharks to someone as cold and inhuman as you are! At least, they're acting according to nature!"

"Oh, and would you prefer me to act more naturally? Have you stopped to consider a man's natural reaction when he finds a girl swimming nude on an empty beach?"

"Stop it!" She put her hands over her ears, as if the act could erase the mocking, gravelly voice. "You have no right to speak to me that way! It's your own fault for sneaking up on me, for following me in the first place! How was I to know there was anyone else there?"

"I have any rights I choose to exercise on this island and it would be a good thing for you to keep in mind," he said coolly. "As for following you, you overrate your allure. The plain fact is, I was planning on having a swim, myself, and I was not particularly pleased to find my privacy already invaded."

"You and your precious privacy! You could have gone somewhere else! It's not as though that were the only water within a dozen miles!"

"In case you hadn't noticed the well-worn track and the chiseled steps, that's the only reasonably safe beach in the vicinity. At any rate, I've lost my taste for swimming, so get along, if you don't mind. You still have a meal to prepare . . . that is if the kitchen has been de-contaminated after your stupid actions earlier."

She had little choice but to follow the trail through the damp underbrush, its outlines fading in the steadily deepening shadows. Her shoes were chaffing before she had gone a hundred feet but she steeled herself not to reveal her discomfort. His relentless footfalls were right behind her and she swung homeward with an angry stride, stiff legged in her anger, her wet hair flapping limply about her shoulders. Even as the surface of it dried on the soft evening air, tendrils danced over to tickle her face and she swiped at them with an impatient hand.

"Here. You were about to lose this," Smith said from behind her.

When she turned, he extended her bra to her and she snatched it out of his hand with a gasp, then turned and began to run. It didn't last. As sore as her pride was, her feet were even sorer and she had to slow down.

"A little late for pretended indignation, isn't it?" he asked derisively. "Don't tell me that crew you were with insisted on full fancy dress whenever they jumped overboard. Or is it the bra? Not much to be embarrassed about there, is there? Your size is not all that impressive, although the conformation is something else again."

His mocking amusement whipped at her and she stalked away, willing her agonized feet to carry her far and fast. His long legs kept

pace with her shorter ones with ease and he
seemed determined to rub salt into her wounded
pride.

"Come on, cut the indignant maiden act. You
forget, I saw you with that crew of Harris's.
They're notorious up and down the coast for
providing entertainment for kids with more
money than morals."

Through gritted teeth, Leah spoke without
turning around or breaking her stride. "The fact
that I was *with* them doesn't necessarily make
me *like* them," she seethed. "Circumstances
aren't always what they seem." She didn't know
why she bothered; his mind was made up and
besides, it didn't matter a hill of beans what he
thought of her. She'd survive his opinion!

"I'll admit you look like an unfledged pullet
but then I've long since learned not to be de-
ceived by appearances. Watch your step!" He
reached out to catch her when she tripped over
her own shoestring and she slithered out from
under his hand and sank to the ground.

"If you hadn't insisted I wear these things,
I wouldn't be hobbling around on blisters the
size of featherbeds!" She grimaced, easing the
shoes off her protesting feet. The relief was
excruciating and she closed her eyes and let her
breath escape through clenched teeth.

He tipped her shoulders back with one hand so
that he could see the damage and she had a
quick, unworthy feeling of smug satisfaction at
the look of consternation that spread over his
face. Before he could say anything though, she
was on her feet, swinging jauntily along the path

in front of him. She might suffer later on, but she wasn't going to show any weakness where Smith Cairington was concerned!

By the time she came out of her bath after showering off the salt water, there was a first aid box open on her dresser with salve and Band-Aids already laid out. She wondered briefly what he would do if she asked his assistance, but after patting herself dry and dressing in white jeans and a brown rib-knit top, she administered to her poor feet and settled for a pair of sandals that missed the worst places. Lazarus! she thought wryly, glancing down at the spotty results.

Waiting for her in the kitchen were three small spanish mackerel, their black and golden eyes already growing dull. Evidently man the provider had not reached the age of chivalry, she decided as she took knife in hand and tried to remember what she had seen on board the *Reef Runner* when Bryce or Toby flipped a freshly caught fish on deck and with a deft flick of a knife, turned it into two neat fillets.

Chapter Four

The fish dinner was more or less a success mainly because Smith came into the kitchen, freshly showered, while Leah was running them under the broiler. She had hacked at the carcasses until she could lift away ragged fillets and it was fortunate that there were no scales to be removed, for she had completely forgotten that step until, with a great feeling of accomplishment, she held up two handsful of firm, gray flesh.

Her hands bore the marks of fins, bones and knife and they pained almost unbearably as she rubbed salt, pepper and lime juice into the meat, according to the instructions in the open cookbook. She melted the butter, smoking it only slightly, and guessed at the distance from broiler to flame, peeping into the open door every thirty seconds until she heard the kitchen door open behind her.

"They smell good enough to eat," Smith remarked laconically.

Glancing up to watch his face as he sampled the aroma, she was glad the odor of perfume had finally dispersed. She had to agree that the fish smelled better.

Smith supervised the turning and taking up of the entree while Leah topped off the salad. At the last minute, she pulled a loaf of Italian bread from the freezer, broke it apart and placed it in a basket. There was no dessert but there were a few kiwi fruits and plenty of apples left and there was a good Stilton cheese to serve with the coffee.

Placing both hands on the table, Leah leaned back with a satisfied smile on her face.

"I think we can both feel justly proud of that one," Smith declared, then, seeing her slightly indignant expression, "well, I *did* catch them, you know, even if you did all the rest."

She relaxed slightly. "I had forgotten about that," she admitted ruefully.

Smith lifted an eyebrow and tipped his chair back as he surveyed her, amusement shining from his eyes.

And then the amusement disappeared, as if a cloud had covered the sun unexpectedly and he reached across the table and picked up one of her hands, turning it to examine the reddened places that marred the lightly tanned skin.

"Good heavens, you're not very deft, are you? These must be giving you the very devil."

Leah pulled her hand away, far more aware of his touch than the vague discomfort of her pricks and cuts. "I may be inept with a knife and a fish, but there *are* things I can do well, thank you."

"Name one," he challenged derisively.

Avoiding the issue, she stood and told him she'd bring coffee into the other room. They were dining in a small corner of the large living room beside sliding glass doors that, in warmer weather would remain open onto a broad porch. She watched his reflection in the glass as he shrugged and moved away. Their pleasant moments seldom lasted long and she didn't honestly know whether it was due to his impatient, condescending attitude or her own defensiveness. Both, probably.

While Leah nibbled her cheese and sipped coffee, Smith studied a diagram of some esoteric piece of machinery that he had spread out on the coffee table. Determined not to break the silence, she stared around the room, taking in such details as the tropical printed linen that covered goosedown cushions. It repeated the vines and flowers outside in a clever way and Leah wondered, not for the first time, about the woman who had designed the interior . . . the woman who fitted the smaller of the two wing chairs that flanked the long sofa.

Putting aside his diagram with an air of having reached some conclusion, Smith Cairington caught her studying him and before she could turn away, their eyes tangled and held. The room seemed vast and empty all of a sudden and it occurred to Leah that they were the only two living beings within who knows how many miles, hardly a comforting thought!

"Do you . . . will we have fish again tomorrow night?" she stammered, more for something to say than because of any real interest.

"Perhaps. The oysters here are magnificent, or I might teach you to dig for pipis," he told her.

"Pipis?"

"A tiny shellfish you chop and fry in a batter."

"Oh."

"Oh," he repeated mockingly. "But before that, I'm afraid you'll have to do a laundry. Either that or we resort to a more informal mode of dress."

He got up and crossed the room to make himself a drink, nor did he bother to offer her anything. Not that she wanted it.

The washing. Another challenge. She went out to the kitchen to tackle the dishes and afterwards, wandered into the utility room to take the measure of the rectangular, enigmatic machine she'd have to cope with the next day. It told her little. There were a few controls on the top and a diagram inside the lid that meant less than nothing to someone who had done no more than rinse out her underclothes in a basin in her room each night.

Well, live and learn, they said. If there was anything she needed to know, no doubt he'd tell her about it before zero hour; meanwhile, she'd just as soon turn in. It had been another long day, filled with some mortifying failures, a moderate success and an incident that did not bear dwelling on. She'd do without swimming from now on rather than risk exposing herself to Smith Cairington's ridicule again.

It was not his ridicule, however, that she remembered long after she went to bed, her eyes open to the warm darkness. Ridicule and contempt were one thing, and she had probably asked for it, even if inadvertently, but the glimmer of something else she had seen in his eyes there on the sheltered beach had been neither of those things; it had been something that she remembered even now with a small, fluttery feeling at the pit of her stomach.

"Mr. Cairington, the eggs are getting low," she announced the next morning as he joined her for breakfast. "Is there a way to get more?"

"Save them for your baking," he told her carelessly. "I think I told you I prefer steak, potatoes and fruit for breakfast."

Leah's mouth dropped open in dismay. Until a day or so ago, the most she had ever done was scrambleds and toast. Now, here she was tossed in at the deep end without a life preserver! She bit back her suggestion as to what he could do with his steak and potatoes. "About the washer. Is there anything I should know about it before I begin?"

He looked up in faint surprise. "Not that I know of. It's a portable, of course. Just roll it in, hook up the hoses and you're off. Right one's hot, left is cold. Powders and bleach are on the shelf beside it and from the looks of the weather, you won't need to worry about drying them. That sun promises to hold out all day."

Smith disappeared immediately after his breakfast, leaving Leah to munch on a piece of toast while she studied her gleaming white opponent. It rolled easy enough . . . right hose hot, left hose cold and a pushbutton that said "start." She finished off the dishes and put them away, clearing the decks so to speak, for her task, and after selecting from among the assorted boxes of laundry detergents, she went off to collect the things to be washed.

Smith's room was larger than hers, furnished in a warm brown with cooling touches of white and turquoise against the satiny paneling. While not a particularly feminine room, it was not exclusively masculine, either. She wondered who usually shared it with him. There were two closets and she had opened them both yesterday morning when she made the beds, closing them almost immediately, aghast at her own curiosity, but not before she had seen the pastel dresses and tailored trouser suits in the largest one. There was a faint but pervasive aroma of jasmine, too, and she had noticed that Smith's aftershave was crisply masculine; mossy with a hint of spice, a mixture she found disconcertingly exciting.

None of my business, she shrugged, stripping the linens from the king-sized bed and gathering up the personal garments from the hamper. She added her own things and pushed aside the disturbing questions as she studied the diagrams on the inner lid of the washing machine. They were worn away on one side, unfortunately, but when she connected up the hoses, remembering which was which, and pushed the button, the machine began to fill in a satisfactory manner.

It was ridiculously easy. The detergent box told her how much to use and she decided not to risk bleach. No point in pushing her luck. With the suds billowing nicely and the paddle churning away, she stared in a bemused way at her peach colored T-shirt going round and round with a pair of Smith's brown pajama pants, then slammed the lid firmly and settled down with her required reading: the cookbook.

She read generalities and specifics on steak and turned to leg of lamb, having first determined the contents of several ambiguous packages in the freezer. It all sounded simple enough and she went on to decide on a foolproof menu for dinner, becoming so engrossed she failed to notice the changed tenor of the background noise. It was not until she felt something warm and wet caressing her bare foot that she pulled her attention away from the various herbs with which one could dress garden peas. By then she was almost ankle deep in suds, with more cascading from the fibrillating section of bent, black hose beside the washer.

"Oh, help! Smith!" she screamed, slamming the book down and swishing her way to the washer. She twisted the faucets frantically but still the deluge continued unabated and she yelled, panic thinning her voice, through the back door.

"Coming, coming," he replied with infuriating calm as he appeared around the corner of the house. "Now, what's got you all excited?"

"It's exploded or something! Come on, make it stop!" Leah held the door open and gestured frantically, grabbing his arm as soon as he got within range to pull him through the door.

It was pure slapstick and in any other circumstance, Leah would have been the first to appreciate it, but as she kicked the side of the machine and pounded on it with her fists, Smith picked up the end of the offending hose and deliberately hooked it over the edge of the sink, where it continued to disgorge its contents harmlessly down the drain.

"You didn't hook it securely enough," he told her witheringly.

"Hook what where?"

"Hook the drainhose into the sink!"

"You didn't even tell me there *was* a drain hose," she wailed.

"Didn't . . . well, you little idiot, what did you think it was, a black snake?"

"How did I know what it was? It was all twisted up behind the machine and I thought it belonged there! Why couldn't you have told me about it?"

He made an inarticulate sound in the back of his throat and pushed a wave of suds aside with his stained canvas shoe. "Can't you do one single thing right? You're without a doubt the most incompetent, irresponsible, in——!"

"Shut up!"

He stepped closer and grabbed her wrist with crippling force. "Don't you tell me to shut up, you little fool! I've done my best to be patient with you and heaven knows, I'd have been smarter to throw you to the fish, but stupid or not, you'll keep a civil tongue in your head when you address me, or I'll peel the hide from your bones!"

She hit bottom then. There wasn't a single thing she could say to refute the charges and when she became aware of the burning blisters on her feet, now thoroughly soaked with hot suds, it was the last straw. She bawled. Her face crumpled and her shoulders slumped and noisy sobs shook her as she stood there, suspended from his hateful grip with not a shred of pride left to hang onto.

"Oh no, not that," Smith groaned, pulling her roughly against him.

Without even the strength left to resist, Leah allowed herself the unlikely comfort of his hard, warm chest and inhaled the sunwashed, slightly musky scent of him between sobs. Finally, she drew a shuddering breath and stiffened herself to pull away. For just an instant it seemed that he wouldn't even allow her that privilege, for his arms tightened almost imperceptibly before he released her.

"Sorry," she breathed raggedly, mopping ineffectually at her wet face with the backs of her hands.

"Yes, well . . . apologies on this end, too. My diplomacy and tact leave something to be desired on occasion." He handed her his handkerchief. "Mop up . . . face first, then we'll tackle the floor. At least it won't need a scrubbing for a while," he finished, allowing her time to adjust her breathing and make repairs to her ravaged face.

There followed a brisk sweeping out and drying up of the floor and a lesson in the proper operation of the portable washing machine, followed by a rather biting remark about the proper pegging of a shirt to the line.

"Left to your own devices, you'd probably tie the sleeves to the clothes pole."

In no mood to take offense, Leah followed him meekly to the back door, bringing the bag of pegs while he carried the bright red plastic basket. At the door, he halted and looked pointedly down at her feet.

"Shoes," he said.

"I really prefer to go barefooted." Especially when her blisters kept being aggravated by first one thing, then another, she added to herself.

"I told you, I'm taking no chances on your stepping on something and getting infected. You're accident prone and I don't intend cutting my stay here short just to get you to the hospital."

"What about your famous flying doctor service?" she argued.

"Would you care to select a landing site? Now be a good girl and put on your shoes, will you?"

"In case you'd forgotten, it was the shoes you

insisted I wear yesterday that got me in this fix in the first place! My feet hurt!"

She marched past him, jaw out-thrust, and got as far as the bottom step before he hooked a hand into her arm and brought her to a jarring halt. "All right, Missy, we'll have a look. I take it you were no better at first aid than you are at anything else." He put the basket down on the small stoop and without straightening up, snatched one of Leah's ankles, tipping her foot to a position where he could see it better. The fact that he almost tipped her, as well, was of no consequence, she thought as she grabbed hold of the wooden bannister.

"You're a right mess, I'll say that for you. If there's a way to do something wrong, you'll find it," he muttered, putting down her left foot to pick up her right.

Smith insisted on marching her back to the bathroom medicine chest where he personally annointed her angry blisters, this time with an antiseptic that stung abominably instead of the bland, soothing ointment she had used. If he had expected to enjoy her discomfort, she foiled him, for she gritted her teeth and closed her eyes and concentrated on not making a sound. As a reward, when he put her well plastered foot back on the floor and stood up, he gave her a pat on the head that made her feel about five years old.

"All finished, so now, how about finding something that doesn't rub the plasters off and we'll get those clothes on the line before winter sets in," he remarked with outrageous cheerfulness.

She settled for the sandals and waited for him

to leave while she put them on. Instead, he leaned against the wall and surveyed her room, taking in the one suitcase she had unpacked and the others, still on the floor. Buckling on the last shoe, she glared up at him.

"I hope you're satisfied!"

"Don't blame me if you're turning out to. be even more of a liability than I'd expected, and that's saying a lot," he shrugged.

"You don't have to keep me, you know! It would suit me just fine if you'd take me to the nearest point of civilization and drop me off! I can think of a few more promising prospects than spending my life slaving away for an oaf who doesn't have the common decency to tell me where the drain hose should go!"

At that he threw back his head and roared. "Oh, you've certainly got your priorities right side up, haven't you? Come on. If you've got those undersized underpinnings of yours squared away, we'll get on with the job at hand and then, to make up for my lamentable lack of bedside manner, I'll give you a treat, all right?"

She stalked out behind him, but by the time the last pillowslip was pegged to the line, her buoyant spirits had rebounded. On a day when the wind chased the marshmallow clouds over a jeweled sea, who could be unhappy? And besides, her feet really did feel heaps better.

The treat was a picnic. With Smith making man-sized sandwiches while Leah put together cheese, fruit, and drinks, they were ready in short order and she followed him past the garden to where the bushtrack separated into two leads. The first went to the coral pool and she had no notion of returning there anytime soon . . . certainly not in his company! They took the other turn and after several minutes of pacing through the shadowy pines, they turned off again and within fifteen minutes or so, they came to a tiny pool fed by a miniature waterfall. Red ladder-ferns caught and rechanneled the water along the edges and a variety of small wildflowers lent a fading, late-summer sweetness to the air.

"You may cool off here anytime you wish in perfect safety, but if you have a hankering to swim, there's hardly room for more than three consecutive strokes. All the same, it's one of my favorite places on the island," he admitted, dropping a cotton blanket onto the dried grass.

"It's wonderful," she conceded. "I didn't know there was anything like this on the island."

"There's more than you'd be able to see in a week of steady exploring, actually, and if you run out of places to discover, we're not all that distant from several smaller islands. In fact, some of them are reachable on foot at low tide."

"If . . . if we're going to be here long enough, I'd like to explore," she said shyly, casting a sidelong glance to see how he took her implied question.

He ignored it. "They're all deserted, of course, but from one end of this coral reef to the other, we have a pretty amazing variety of flora and fauna."

As if to prove his words, a large black swallow-tailed bird with a red patch on his throat swooped over the clearing, protesting the intrusion. "Frigate bird," Smith told her, digging into the lunch bag for his first sandwich.

They spent an hour munching and talking desultorily. There were countless questions jostling for position in Leah's mind but she was wary of breaking the precarious peace between them. Smith identified the birds that flew into range and named the flowers whose names he knew . . . a short list, at best, and one whose accuracy she doubted when he came up with such gems as "John's-Other-Slipper" and "Maiden's Loss." When she challenged him he merely grinned and closed his eyes against the lowering sun, his head pillowed on crossed arms.

The silence was filled with rustlings and the distant cries of birds, as well as with the gentle sound of the falling water. It had a lulling effect and as her eyes rested on the form of the sleeping man beside her, Leah realized that she was not at all unhappy at the unexpected turn of events. She could soon learn to cope with the housekeeping details . . . after all, she was not a stupid person, merely inexperienced. The thing was, could she cope with living in close contact with a man she was beginning to find physically attractive . . . enormously attractive? It would be the height of folly to find herself falling in love with a man she didn't even particularly like, she thought as her eyes strayed over the high, broad shape of his chest to the lean, flat hips and the long, muscular legs. The lightweight khaki pants concealed without necessarily disguising the man beneath and Leah felt an odd stirring that had nothing at all to do with rational thought.

She had little enough reason to like the man; all the same, she was learning that there were various shadings to the word, like, some she had never before experienced. Tantalizing, half-formed ideas floated to the surface of her mind and when a leaf drifted down to rest on Smith's cheek, causing him to stir, she was glad to escape her own vagarious mind by breaking into speech.

"You don't live here year round, do you, Mr. Cairington?"

His eyes opened so easily she wondered uncomfortably if he had been awake all the time, aware of her interest under the screen of thick, dark lashes that guarded those clear, gray eyes. "No, I don't. Why do you ask?"

She shrugged her shoulders, unusually sensitive to the feel of soft cotton against her bare skin. "No real reason, I guess. You were obviously coming from somewhere when you . . . when I . . ."

He rescued her. "I live most of the time in Melbourne. Any other questions seething beneath the surface of that deceptively calm facade of yours?" A quirk of a smile robbed the words of any real sting and she took him up on his offer before he changed his mind.

"What do you do? What's your family like? How many times do you come here and how long do you stay? Who else . . ."

"Whoa! Back up, girl," he laughed, rolling over onto his side to face her. She was sitting crosslegged, chewing a stem of grass and she felt his teasing smile flow over her like a warm wind. She returned it with one of her own, perhaps the most open, generous smile she had permitted herself in all too long.

"First, I suppose I'm what you might call a jack-of-all-trades. Dealings in wool, tin, and beef, primarily, holding together the odds and ends accumulated by my father and his father, plus various family connections through the years. Family? Let's see . . . father deceased, mother remarried, two brothers, younger, one sister, older, half a dozen assorted aunts, uncles and cousins, all more or less respectable."

He spoke jokingly but all the same, Leah's smile became slightly strained.

"I come here maybe two, three times a year," he continued, "and as for how long I stay, well, that depends on a number of things." He eyed her speculatively and she was somewhat surprised to note that, while his expression held no real acceptance, at least the contempt was gone.

"Your turn now," he told her after the silence had hung there long enough.

"Well," Leah began with mock gravity, "you might say I'm a jill-of-all-trades . . . washing, cooking . . ." She rolled away as he swatted her lazily. "Dealing in lamb chops and drainages, primarily," she giggled.

"Family?" he prompted, bringing about an instant sobering of her delicate features.

"One great aunt, name of Harriet Stevens,

one stepmother, name of Katherine Deerfield, in the process of becoming an un-step when . . . when it became unnecessary," she finished unevenly. She didn't add Delia's name to the list because she had never considered the girl in the light of a stepsister.

"The States . . . northern part, I'd guess."

She eyed him curiously. "How can you tell?"

"The accent. It's not quite so free wheeling as our own."

"You know the States?" she ventured cautiously.

"Reasonably well," he said, confirming her fears. "Cairington's has offices in New York and London which require occasional visits . . . frequent ones lately."

"Then you've . . . been over in the past year?"

He named a month that sent a tight, wary look to her face and she turned away, gathering up the remains of the picnic. It was entirely possible that he'd never even heard of Justin Deerfield. After all, what interest could a New York stock manipulation scandal have for an Australian businessman?

"Justin Deerfield?" he asked gently, addressing her cameolike profile as she twisted the paper sack in her hands.

She lifted her head to stare unseeingly at a gull that wheeled overhead, bracing herself for the inevitable. Half a world away and still she couldn't outrun it. She nodded her head as she started to rise to her feet and he caught her hand, pulling her off balance. She toppled awkwardly, sprawling half across his chest, her mouth open to protest angrily.

"Does it matter so much to you, Leah?" he asked softly, holding her in place with an arm across her shoulders. He searched her face with eyes that suddenly looked as warm as the sunlight on the bark of a karaka tree.

"Of course it matters to me! He was my father, after all, no matter what he did . . . they said he did!" Her hastily summoned defenses were in danger of crumpling under his unexpected gentleness and she struggled to rise. "He wasn't a bad person, Mr. Cairington, no matter what people said."

"It never occurred to me that he was, Leah. Men don't reach Justin Deerfield's position of trust without having their integrity tested time and time again. He passed all but the last test, my dear, and we'll probably never know what happened to change him at the end."

She sat silently for a long time, dwelling on his words. She was only dimly aware of the hand that held her own, a thumb idly rubbing the blemished skin on its surface. When she spoke it was to say that she had never really known her father in any case.

Under Smith's skilled handling, she went on to reveal more of her childhood than she realized, up to and including the latest episodes of being shifted from place to place. She made no effort to excuse herself for not being able to stand on her own two feet at an age when most girls were self-supporting and he didn't comment, one way or another. But then, it didn't really concern him, so why should he bother to voice an opinion? The fact that he had already voiced more than one, all distinctly unflattering, did not occur to her at the moment, and if it had, she would not have made much of it. It was enough that he had allowed her to spill out all the churning doubts of the past year or so, something she had not allowed herself to do before. Maybe time lent a certain objectivity to the whole affair; whatever the cause, Leah felt better than she had in ages, as if she'd shed a burden she had dragged around with her until it had become a part of her.

Suddenly becoming embarrassed by her own outpourings, she sought an impersonal topic. "Mr. Cairington, there's a cloud coming over the treetops. I'd hate to have all those things on the line soaked again."

With a smile that made her wonder why she had ever thought him not handsome, Smith pulled her to him in a light, playful hug. He was still lying on his back and her head fell naturally into the hollow of his shoulder. "I think we've graduated to first names, don't you? Besides, I've already been Smith to you once today."

"When was that?" she demanded, struggling to glare at him from her prone position.

"When you ran screaming out of the kitchen chased by a sudsy monster," he retorted, and before she could fathom his intent, he placed his mouth over hers in a salute that was both more and less than a kiss.

His mouth, stunningly soft for all its look of

harshness on occasion, barely touched her own before lifting to remain a breath away. His eyes stayed open, as did her own, and she could see herself reflected clearly in the twin silver lakes.

"Why did you do that?" she whispered breathlessly.

"Why not?" he shrugged after only a moment's hesitation.

Chapter Five

If she suffered a few bad nights it was not because she hadn't worn herself out during the daylight hours. The week that followed was crowded with activity, or as crowded as Leah could make it. There was a satisfyingly increasing number of modest triumphs as well as some resounding failures; among the latter was the birthday cake.

She had gone out of her way to avoid Smith, suspecting her own weakness where he was concerned. While she was still not safe from his quick temper, the fact that he could be so unexpectedly kind on occasion threatened to disarm her entirely.

To her chagrin, he seemed equally intent on avoiding her. The net needed relining, a slow and tedious matter, and then there was the *Sunfisher* . . . something about installing a new navigational system. Whatever the reason, Leah was more than a little put out, for it was one thing to choose solitude for herself, quite another to have it wished upon her.

Smith did, however, show her how to dig the oval shelled pipis and mince them and they searched out a recipe for batter. After having to discard the first batch, she became adept at frying up the golden, succulent fritters and they fell back on them whenever the fish refused to bite.

It was when she was passing the library-cum-office that she heard him talking to someone through the closed door. She had been on her way to his bedroom with a stack of freshly, if inexpertly ironed shirts and trousers and her steps slowed at the sound in spite of herself.

"Eden, this is Chance, come in, come in," his voice intoned through the thin wood of the door.

"Hullo there, Chance, this is Eden, come back?"

"Righto, Eden, old dear, how've you been keeping?" Smith's voice held a note of joviality that Leah had never heard before and she absently rubbed one ankle with a bare foot as she stood poised, subduing a feeling of something suspiciously like jealousy. Eden sounded very female, whoever she was, and more than a little fond.

"Has our shipment arrived yet?" Smith continued.

Shipment? It was a business call, then, Leah decided with relief.

"Expecting it any day now, Chance, and from the word around here, you did well to play switcheroo."

"I thought as much. Listen, Eden, if there's anything going on that can't be delegated, just get on the blower at the time we agreed on, right? Otherwise, the timetable stands."

"Righto, love. Meanwhile, I can't let you go without wishing you many happy returns. If I were there I'd do you a giant pavlova, complete with slices of kiwi and a gaudy candle. Wouldn't you just adore it?" There was a teasing note in the slightly husky voice, as if Eden, whoever she was, knew him exceedingly well.

Many happy returns! That must mean today was Smith's birthday! She missed the sign-off completely and only the sound of those firm footsteps crossing the room moved her from the spot. She darted into the bedroom and dropped his laundry on the foot of his bed as if it were too hot to handle. Let him put his own things away; she had done her part. Her hands were decorated with dark reddish blemishes from the unaccustomed task. It was shameful in this day of permanent press to have to spend hours over a hot ironing board, but she was not about to risk his censure for a task half done; she received more than enough of his criticism as it was, without seeking it.

With lunch out of the way, she set to with a will. The cookbook gave several variations of a favorite Australian dessert called pavlovas but none looked as scrumptious as the traditional birthday cake pictured at the front of the chapter on desserts. She decided on chocolate over a golden batter and got down to it. Half the time she had to refer to the glossary for an interpretation of terms and she lost her place frequently in the process, but by midafternoon she was putting the finishing touches on an unbelievably gorgeous product. The script she had planned for the top went wrong and after several attempts, she settled for waves and a lopsided starfish with the initials, S.C., in the center.

She hid the cake in the pantry and gathered up the enormous number of utensils and put them in to soak while she got to work on a foolproof menu, using one of the frozen casseroles and a salad with both cooked and raw vegetables. The recipes were becoming easier to interpret all the time and with any luck at all, she might leave this island a fairly creditable cook. Who knows, perhaps her future awaited her in some hamburger palace!

Tonight, in view of the celebration, she decided to wear a dress. For some reason she never fully explored, she had stuck to jeans and casual shirts, but there was no reason why she shouldn't make use of some of the lovely things her father had bought her after graduation from St. Genevieve's.

By the time she had selected a bottle of rosé from among those in the rack the casserole was beginning to send out tantalizing hints of joys to come. She hurried out and selected a polished cotton of blue and green print that made her eyes almost jadelike instead of the more prosaic hazel. She piled her hair up into a loose knot and allowed the short, curly new growth free reign, admiring the way it glistened with new, sun-induced gold against the mousy brown. She went as far as to use a touch of lipgloss and reached for the perfume, but decided against it. What was it he had said? A second rate bordello? What, pray tell, would a first rate one be like, considering the price of her tiny flacon of French perfume?

She felt more than a little self-conscious pouring the wine and she looked up when Smith came in, showered and dressed in white pants and a brown knit shirt. He stopped dead in his tracks and stared at her, which didn't make things any more comfortable, before placing his half empty whiskey on the sideboard.

"Well, well, well," he said softly and expressively. "What have you been hiding under wraps all this time?"

His indulgent tone had the effect of taking the curse off her own embarrassment, for some reason, and she grinned at him. "It's all too easy to forget the rules," she told him, thinking of the tight, circumscribed evening meals at school with a member of the faculty at each table. "Spine straight, spoon away from your body and . . ."

"And square your soup, or was that only in military academies?"

They laughed together and Leah was aware of his appreciative glance taking in her bared arms and the cut of her dress as it shaped her small breasts. Perhaps it had been a mistake to call attention to her femininity, under the circumstances.

"Sit down and I'll bring the casserole," she said hurriedly, hiding her fluster under a cloak of practicality.

The meal went off without a hitch and Smith even complimented her on her choice of wines.

"I couldn't go far wrong, choosing from among the chosen."

"No, probably not, all the same, this is just the touch. The salad is . . . different," he remarked.

She looked up worriedly. "Does that mean you don't like it?"

"Of course not, you silly goose. You've improved by leaps and bounds. You'll notice my clean plate?"

"There was room for improvement," she offered ruefully as he started to rise from the table. "No, not yet. There's more."

She hurried off to the pantry and returned almost immediately bearing dessert plates and the magnificent cake. Candles would have been nice, but she hadn't found any. Anyway, with the lights on, the decorations showed up to a better advantage.

Smith slowly pushed back his chair and stood, his eyes riveted to her offering. From there, his eyes moved up to take in her painfully

proud expression and his face seemed almost
to crumple into a smile that made her want to
weep.

"My very dear girl, how on earth did you
know?" he asked softly.

"I overheard you talking," she admitted. "I
didn't mean to eavesdrop, it was just that I
couldn't imagine who you were talking to and I
stopped before I realized what I was doing."

"Not to apologize, child, it was only natural. It
didn't occur to me that you didn't know about
the transceiver. At any rate, I must admit I'm
glad you overheard. I was beginning to feel a bit
sorry for myself . . . neglected, you know. No
wild neckties, no bad cigars."

"Oh, well, I didn't get you a gift," she began,
and he leaned over the table and placed a large
brown hand over hers, covering the knife with
which she had just sliced the cake.

"Please . . . no more apologies, my dear.
You've done something so remarkable . . . so
totally unexpected, that I'll remember this birthday as the most outstanding one for years to
come." He squeezed her hand and let her get on
with the serving.

The texture was slightly uneven, but far better
than she had dared hope. She watched anxiously as he cut into the golden sponge, through the
dark, lush icing, and raised the bit appreciative-
ly to his mouth. She wasn't even aware of having
held her breath until he lowered his fork.

No nuance of expression could have escaped
her then, and so she saw the flicker cross his
face, even though he recovered almost instant-

ly. "What's wrong?" she demanded, staring suspiciously at her own smaller serving.

He shook his head, indicating that he couldn't answer yet and she forked up a bite and tasted it cautiously.

"Yuk!" It was dreadful!

"Not to worry, sweet, we can pour syrup on it, and anyway, the icing is delectable."

"It's terrible!" she wailed. "What went wrong?"

He was around the table before she could move, leaning over her to murmur words that were intended to reassure her but she refused to be comforted.

"I followed the recipe . . . it looks so lovely . . . I can't believe it," she agonized, brushing away his arm as she stood up. "I'll bet it was all those silly tsp's and tbs's!"

Before he realized what she was about, she had swept up the cake on its silver platter and was running to the kitchen door with it. He followed her just in time to see her open the door and hurl the cake out into the darkness. "There!" she cried, "Happy birthday, ants and . . . and b-birds!" Slinging the platter onto the counter, she dashed past him and ran to her room, tears streaming down her face as she gave in to the overwhelming disappointment and embarrassment.

"Leah? Are you all right?" he called softly through the door.

"Go away," she choked, burying her face deeper in the pillow.

The door opened soundlessly behind her and

the first she knew of his presence was a gentle pressure on her heaving shoulders.

"It's only a cake, honey. The rest of the meal was delicious," he murmured against her hair, now sadly awry from twisting on the pillow.

"The rest of the meal was out of the freezer," she sniffed. "Some other woman cooked it, so it doesn't count."

He turned her deftly and without quite knowing how it came about, she found her face pressed against his tobacco brown knit shirt, feeling the hard warmth of his body beneath her cheek. "I . . . I wanted to please you," she whispered shakily, trying surreptitiously to wipe her nose on her hand.

He shifted slightly and produced a handkerchief, one she had ironed that day, no doubt. "Was it so important to please me, then?"

"It's your birthday," she exclaimed, her tones accusing as she stared up at him from drenched eyes. "I would have t-tried a pavlova but I wasn't sure how it would look with happy birthday written on it and anyway, the cake looked so wonderful in the picture."

He laughed then and the sound traveled through Leah's body causing strange little ripples of sensation. "Honey, pavlovas are my least favorite dessert . . . I'm not a dessert man, anyhow, truth be known."

"But she said . . . Eden, that is, that if she were here she'd make you a giant one," she protested.

Another slight shift found them seated side by

side on her bed, leaning back against the black-wood headboard. Smith's arm was still around her and she leaned unashamedly into the hollow of his shoulder. "My family are great practical jokers, Leah. Eve . . . Eden, that is, has built me that pavlova whenever we happened to be together for my birthday and she made sure it was presented in circumstances where I'd be forced to eat a huge chunk and pretend to enjoy it. One of these days, I'll crown her with one of those things!" He laughed indulgently and Leah knew he didn't really mean it.

"Is it Eve or Eden?"

Ruefully, he admitted to the former. "Eve's my sister. We didn't particularly want the world and its brother to know where I was and these radios aren't the most private means of communications, you know."

"And you're so certain the world and its brother watches your every move?" she retorted with a spark of her former vitality.

"Touché," he grinned softly. "The world that has to do with Cairington Enterprises, shall we say?"

"Your brothers, are they practical jokers, too?"

"The world's worse. Matter of fact, I thought at first you were one of their jokes," he confessed.

Leah stiffened and drew away, only to be pulled back relentlessly. "Don't go getting your dander up, young lady," he admonished. "It was a natural mistake and if you knew all the circumstances, you'd be the first to agree. I'll enjoy seeing their faces when they find out about you. They'll kick themselves for not having thought of it in the first place."

Outside, the cicadas had tuned up and Leah felt a warm swelling of peace and contentment. She snuggled deeper into his arm. "I'm not at all sure I like the idea of being someone's practical joke, especially when I don't even know what it's all about. You wouldn't care to enlighten me, I suppose?"

"No, child, I'm afraid not." He rubbed his chin on her hair and she raised her head to study his face, finding it disconcertingly close. "I'm not a child, you know."

"Yes, you are," he said softly, "very much a child and very much my junior and now I think I'd better leave you to clear away in the kitchen. Next thing we know, you'll be wanting time-and-a-half for overtime." The words were spoken lightly but he didn't sound particularly jocular and there was a tightness about his lean cheeks, as if he were clenching his teeth.

Some instinct that was infinitely older than Leah's own few years took over. "With the cake a flop, I didn't really give you anything for your birthday," she told him softly, a question in her gold-shot eyes.

He stiffened without actually moving away. "And just what did you have in mind as a substitute?"

"This," she whispered, raising her face that tiny bit necessary to reach his mouth. Her kiss was butterfly soft and it landed on the corner of his mouth. She didn't want to end it, needing something far more intense from him and not fully understanding what it was.

With a low growl, he took her tentative gesture and turned it into something quite different. His own mouth ground harshly into her soft lips and he reached up and clasped her chin, jerking it downward to open her mouth to his seeking. The combination of ruthless force and practiced skill were more than a match for Leah's inexperience and by the time he raised his head, she was a limp, trembling mass of pure longing.

"Maybe from now on you'll behave yourself," he jeered, pushing her away to get to his feet. When she didn't speak, he turned to stare down at her, his expression veiled.

Totally incapable of hiding her emotions, Leah could only gaze back at him, her mouth soft and swollen and her eyelashes still tangled from earlier tears. There was no accusation in her eyes, only puzzlement, a bewildered sort of hurt that brought an instant tightening to his own face.

He reached for her hand. "Leah, I'm sorry. That was an unforgivable thing to do, but you must know you just can't take a man into your bed and kiss him and—"

"I didn't take you into my bed," she reminded him huskily. "You followed me here . . . I didn't invite you."

He dropped back down beside her, then stood up again abruptly, still clutching her hand in a crippling grip.

"My hand," she whispered, tugging at her fingers, "You're hurting me."

He dropped it immediately, then, with a look of consternation, picked it up again. "What happened now? These are new!" He examined the darkened patches that marred her hands, perhaps half a dozen places in all.

"I've never done all that much ironing," she admitted with a watery smile. "I'm about as expert at that as I am at cooking and washing."

"Ahhhh." The breath seemed to leave his body in a soft sigh and he raised her hands to his lips, touching her burns tenderly. It hurt, but of course, she'd die before letting him know that.

"They're only tiny places. They stung for a little while but now they're all right," she assured him, trying not to wince at his touch.

His tongue touched the wide place on her knuckle and then her little finger found its way into the soft warmth of his mouth and she closed her eyes against the sensations that sprang up inside her, pain the very least of them.

"I'll wash up tonight, my dear." he told her. "The touch of anything wet on these would be agony." He looked down at her with concern and then, with a widening of realization in his eyes, he threw her hand from him, muttered a curse and left the room, slamming the door behind him.

Leah was strangely reluctant to get out of bed the next morning and it took several minutes for the memory of the past evening to unfold itself. When it did, she groaned and pushed her head back into the pillow, resisting an impulse to pull the covers over her head. How could she have been such a little fool? Who could blame the man for slamming out of her bedroom as if all the furies were pursuing him? She had had him in her bed in all innocence and she, herself, had changed it into something else. It was Leah, herself, who had instigated that kiss; she had raised her lips to his mouth in what she thought was a simple birthday salute . . . or did she? Wasn't she deliberately deluding herself? Hadn't she been aware of his masculinity beside her? If not when she raised her face to his, certainly within seconds when he took her at her own invitation and deepened her chaste salute to something quite different.

Even now her face burned at the memory. And her hands . . . his tongue on her wounds, the feel of the soft, moist warmth on her fingers . . .

"Ahhh, darn!" she muttered softly dragging herself out of bed.

It took all the time between showering and making her bed to brace herself for walking out into the kitchen as if nothing untoward had happened. She had caught sight of her face in the medicine chest mirror and searched for any obvious signs of difference. There were none; the same high, rather childish forehead, the untidy light brown hair curling around it, the same short, slender nose over a mouth that was neither large nor small . . . just a plain mouth, she told herself, totally unconscious of her own innocent allure. There was certainly nothing of the femme fatale in that set of features, she decided wryly, knowing she didn't look much different from when she was fifteen, but when, on stepping out of the shower, she encountered her image in the door mirror, she stopped and stared.

This was no child's body. Oh, no, there might not be very much of it, but it was definitely female, definitely woman . . . and this was the body Smith had seen floating unashamed on top of the coral pool that first day on the island!

She chose her loosest pair of jeans to step into and pulled on a baggy sweat shirt that owed its place in her favor more to comfort than to looks. Seeing again the slender line of her jaw, she thrust out her chin in a no-nonsense manner and pushed open her bedroom door, marching directly into the kitchen with the light of battle in her eyes.

It was empty. There were signs of Smith's having foraged for himself and the jar of instant coffee was still open, but he had gone and she felt her bravado fade before a wave of guilt. He had told her that first day he liked a big breakfast and she had used any excuse she could manufacture to avoid breaking out that mammoth grill until a few days ago. Since then he had suffered her attempts in stoic silence and she was reminded all over again of how very patient he had been. After all, she owed him her room and board, her passage, too, although she might have preferred to have a say in her destination, in that case.

Not that Chance Island was a bad place to have fetched up. It was, all in all, a great experience, and she admitted to having learned more in a few short weeks than she had in the past few years, but all the same, from now on, there'd be none of the easy familiarity they had lapsed into on occasion. She had seen the dangers inherent in that! From now on, it was strictly employer, employee.

The grill mastered, she tackled biscuits or as Smith called them scones, and, after throwing away a dozen or so, to the delight of the gulls, she succeeded in improving all out of reason. Smith was appreciative, but only in the most impersonal sort of way. He seemed even more determined than Leah to put their relationship on a strictly business footing and once more, she found herself slightly piqued when he persisted in taking himself off after every meal and remaining until time for the next. Having made the very same resolution herself, she would have liked to have been the one to implement it.

Another week passed in which the two of them saw each other only at mealtimes and after dinner, shared a silent sort of companionship in the living room occasionally before she excused herself to go to bed.

Leah had discovered the books in the room with the transceiver, a room that was usually off limits to her since Smith used it for his office as well as his regular transmissions. She helped herself to several well-seasoned detective stories, and when the printed word no longer held her attention, she allowed her eyes to stray to the other side of the room, where Smith's lean, dark face remained closed to her as he poured over ledgers and diagrams and the occasional novel. He always made a motion to stand and murmured a polite good-night when she excused herself but he showed nothing but a poorly concealed relief at her departure, to her chagrin.

She overheard two more radio transmissions, although she usually found something to occupy her in another part of the house when time came for his regular call to Eden, or Eve, as he openly called her now. The first one was to a man and it concerned something about proxies, a shareholders meeting and a bore going dry and the other one was from his sister. Whatever the parcel Smith had been expecting had arrived in good condition but was deteriorating rapidly and did he want it redirected before it became too difficult to handle?

He did not, thank you very much, and if that were the case, there would be no more radio contact except in case of emergency.

Very much mystified, Leah told herself that it was either another of their practical jokes or else Smith had never outgrown a boyish love of cops and robbers games. She shrugged it off and went her own way, accomplishing her chores in less and less time as she grew more expert, and spending her spare time exploring the island.

Twice she left his lunch prepared and took herself off to the waterfall pool with a book and a bit of fruit and cheese. She made a game of trying to identify trees and birds, but with little luck. Horticulture had never been of particular interest to her and the trees that grew here on the island bore scant resemblance to those with which she was familiar.

She thought often of home, such as it was, wondering if Great Aunt Harriet ever gave a thought to what had become of her. She had stopped writing to her few school friends after the scandal, figuring they would prefer not to know her, and wishing to save them the embarrassment of having to break it off. Most often, she thought of the summer camp and the children she had worked with. If she had left a bit of her heart anywhere, it was there, with the children who had needed and trusted her.

She began to wonder how long Smith intended remaining on the island. There were certain indications that he wouldn't be content to stay forever. Just lately, in fact, he had sunned and repacked all the life jackets and refilled the carboy with fresh water. He had been working nights lately on restoring the frayed lines from the *Sunfisher*, too, and Leah had been fascinated with what he called splicing, but what looked to her like macramé.

"The bowline is pretty badly frayed," he told her one morning when she came on him as he finished splicing an eye into one of the lines. "I'll let you watch me tomorrow when I mend it and then you can try your own hand with something lighter and softer."

After dinner that night, he had dropped a book

on knots and splicing in her lap as he passed through the living room on his way to the library. The smile he gave her, even though he didn't speak, held something of the old camaraderie and she found herself sitting crosslegged in her chair after he had gone, the book clutched to her chest and an inane smile on her face.

Chapter Six

Sometime during the night Leah was awakened by a banging against the side of the house. She sat up and listened, waiting for the noise to repeat itself. There was no sound from the other side of the hallway and she decided Smith must have slept through it, whatever it was. In listening for a sharper sound, she missed the soft moaning of the wind through the treetops until it picked up strength to a wavering shriek.

Slipping out of bed, she padded across her floor to look out into the darkness. Her window was open, for she didn't sleep well in a closed space, and she felt the rain blowing through before she even reached it. Out there in the blustering night, she could hear the surf crashing against the shore and the first thought that crossed her mind was the *Sunfisher* with her chaffed bowline.

There was still no sign that Smith was aware of the change in the weather and she crossed the hallway, half expecting to see a line of light under his door, but it was dark. She crossed to his bed and reached out a hand to shake him awake and despite the fact that her mind was on something other than the man, himself, she felt an odd tingle all the way through her when her hand encountered warm, bare flesh.

"Smith! Wake up! It's storming out there!"

He rolled over heavily and she caught a sudden drift of alcohol. It came as a shock, for although she knew he had a short whiskey before dinner each night, it had never occurred to her that he might have anything more after she retired.

"What is it?" he asked, coming suddenly alert.

"The wind is up and the sea sounds ferocious. I was worried about the boat," she told him, backing away now that he was fully awake. It was too dark to see more than the vaguest shapes; nevertheless, when he threw back the covers, she turned hastily and made her way to the door. "Do you need any help?" she asked from that safe distance.

"No, I don't think so. Get the torch from the kitchen, though, will you? And turn on the yard lights, there's a good girl."

Glad to have a task she hurried away, her thin

cotton gown flapping about her legs as she dashed out to the kitchen.

After Smith had let himself out the back door, Leah watched from the vantage point of the kitchen window. The house lights reached only about halfway down the path to the jetty and although there was a light pole out on the end, it had not worked since they had been on the island, due, Smith told her, to a part that was out of stock.

She followed the wavering yellow eye of the torch as it jogged along the downward path and she could more or less make out his actions from its course. It was perfectly clear to her what had happened when she watched it topple over the edge of the jetty, strike the rail of the *Sunfisher* and sink slowly beneath the surface.

"Leah!" Even over the relentless winds, she could hear his voice.

"I'll bring it!" she answered at the top of her lungs. She didn't have to ask what he needed. She located the second torch and was out the door and halfway down the path before she realized that not only had she not stopped to put on a raincoat, she had not even worn her robe . . . not that it would have done any good! At least she'd have a nice, warm, dry bathrobe to put on when she got back inside.

"Here it is," she panted, handing over the torch.

"Good girl!"

She stood back and when he said, hold this, she held it. When he jumped down into the boat, leaving her alone on the dark jetty with the wind driven rain pelting her skin as if she wore nothing at all, she held her ground, waiting to be told he no longer needed her. The *Sunfisher* heaved at its mooring lines as if it were alive, a creature stranded out of its element and fighting to get back.

By the time Smith jumped lightly back up beside her and tested the new lines, satisfying himself that they were secure, Leah was shivering with cold and excitement.

"Here now, you should have gone back up to the house, child," he exclaimed on feeling her wet, cold flesh. He took her arm and turned her toward the house, making her trot along beside him as he tried to shield her from the worst of the rain. "Not a grain of sense in your head," he muttered, pushing her through the door and slamming it behind him.

Under the pitiless glare of the kitchen fixture, Leah looked down at herself aghast! The white cotton gown might just as well not have been there; the rain had made it all but invisible!

She looked up to see Smith's narrowed eyes and with a gasp, she turned and dashed off to her room, slamming the door behind her. He was two steps behind her, entering without even bothering to knock.

"Get out of here!" she flung at him, caught in the act of lifting the hem of her sodden garment.

"I will, right enough, but you don't just hop into bed like that."

"Do you think I'm crazy? Of course I won't just go to bed like this!"

"What you'll do is climb into a hot tub . . . no,

not your shower, but my tub, and I'll rummage up something to heat you up from the inside."

"I'm perfectly all right! Don't fuss so, for goodness sake," she chattered at him, knowing it was only concern on his part but far too aware of his own drenched form. His khakis clung like a second skin and she was suddenly painfully aware of her own feminine vulnerability. "Would you please get out of here?" she agonized.

Without bothering to answer, he grabbed up her bathrobe, a plain, tailored white silk affair, and clamped her elbow with his other hand. "Come along before you crack those chattering teeth of yours."

She had little choice, for he urged her along as if she were on the verge of pneumonia. He led her through his own room to the bath adjoining and shoved her ungently through the door. "Get at it, then. Steaming hot, and plenty of it. I'll be back in a minute with something to put inside you."

When she opened her mouth to protest, he squelched her with a leveling look. "I told you once, this place is off the beaten track for housecalls and I don't intend to have you falling apart on my hands. Now, hop to it!"

There was a moment of grim amusement when an investigation of the several jars that lined the gleaming tub revealed jasmine-scented bubble bath and talcum. She threw in a generous handful of the former, picturing a masculine creature like Smith Cairington luxuriating in such fragrant suds.

Then, of course, reality set in and she reminded herself that he didn't always visit Chance alone. There were signs aplenty of female occupancy and for all she knew, he might have a wife tucked away somewhere. She frowned and twisted on the hot faucet with her foot, trying to picture the man she knew spending domestic holidays here with a wife and children.

Still, he hadn't mentioned them when she asked about his family. Besides, he didn't seem married.

The door opened and he stuck his head in, following it when he saw her sink beneath the brimming suds. The flush on her face owed as much to indignation as it did to the hot water and she extended a hand impatiently for the glass he held out to her.

"Sherry ought to do the trick for a nondrinker like you. With anything stronger, I might have to come to the rescue and I don't think either of us needs that." His tone was mocking and Leah said the first thing that came to her mind.

"Smith, are you married?"

His eyes widened and he stared down at her. "Am I what?"

"Well, I only asked," she muttered into the softly exploding bubbles on her chest. "You don't exactly seem the sort for jasmine bubbles and I was giving you the benefit of the doubt."

"For your information, young Leah, I have neither wife nor mistress . . . at the moment, nor am I in the market for either." With his hand on the door, he turned back. "And if I were, you can be certain I'd be looking for more experienced applicants than any I've seen lately!" he added meaningfully.

If she could have reached him, she would have wiped that smug expression right off his face! "I'm not . . . I wasn't . . . for *your* information, you insufferably conceited pig, I wouldn't have you on a bet! Not for anything!"

"No? You could have fooled me there a couple of times," he remarked with infuriating calm as he closed the door softly behind him.

Leah needed nothing more to warm her now. She tossed off the sherry in three gulps, made a face and submerged herself in the suds before pulling the plug. It took several minutes of rinsing off to rid herself of the clinging lather and because she was still in a temper, she was not especially neat. There was water everywhere and she tossed her towel down after a few cursory swipes and pulled on her robe. If Smith Cairington had been in his room when she came out, she would have flung the wet towel at him, for she was definitely in a flinging mood.

He was not. Hair dripping down her back, rapidly undoing all the good her hot soak had done her, she stalked down the hallway, flinching as the cool night air struck her overheated body. She returned the glass to the kitchen but would wash it in the morning after she cleaned up his bathroom. At the moment it looked as if the easterly had blown clean through the house and she couldn't care less!

When she opened her own door, a dark figure moved away from her window and she stopped dead in her tracks.

"You left your window open and the floor's awash," he said.

"Then I'll jolly well have to mop it up, shan't I? Will you please get out of here!"

"Tsk tsk, you're far too young for such a temper, Leah child. And I've already mopped up for you."

"I'm not a Leah child or any other kind of child and I don't want you barging into my room when ever you take a notion! If the roof falls in, I'll deal with it, if you please!"

His low laughter set up a reverberation along her spine and she stepped backward with the intention of escaping his presence. There was another bedroom she could use if necessary, with a chair under the doorknob!

"I think you're afraid of me, little Leah," he said, moving to her side with silent swiftness. He caught her by the nape and leaned over to sniff her hair. "Hmmm, jasmine. Always one of my favorites."

"I'll just bet it is! Do you keep a special fragrance for each of your women?" She did her level best to escape his deceptively gentle grip but he only pulled her to him. He had changed into something dry and now she inhaled his own particular scent . . . mossy and a hint of spice.

"Shall I get in a stock of your own favorite?" he mused, nuzzling her throat beneath her collar. "What was it, anyway?"

She stiffened. "That was a very expensive French perfume," she informed him, her voice wavering as she tried to ignore the effect on her nerves of his tiny nibbling kisses.

"I'm sure it was, love, but it was never intended to mingle with incinerated luncheon. Hold still, will you?"

"No, I won't!" she gave one last protest and then surrendered as his mouth closed over hers, his arms coming up to hold her head steady beneath his assault. One arm dropped to her shoulder and then to her waist and her hips, to cradle her frighteningly close against his virile masculinity. "This isn't a good idea at all, you know," he breathed against her throat before returning to plunder her mouth once more.

To her everlasting shame, she didn't want him to stop. Oh, no, it was not a good idea at all, but for now, please let him not stop and she'd worry about tomorrow when it came.

He must have sensed her incipient surrender in the way she clung unashamedly to him. When she felt his hand slip beneath her robe to fire her with his discovering touch, she curved herself to his palm, gasping as she felt her nipple harden to a throbbing probe.

"We can't do this, you know, my precious," he whispered, removing his hand and pulling the edges of her robe back together again.

"Why can't we?" She was beyond shame now, beyond everything except for this brand new, overpowering need he had aroused in her.

"My heavens, child, don't!" he groaned.

"But you started it," she protested, her voice slightly slurred. Her eyelids were growing heavy and there was a burning sensation creeping along her veins, licking tiny flames into a converging inferno in the pit of her stomach.

"I know I . . . you started it just by being here,
if you must know!" He put her from him deliberately now and if there was a slight reluctance in
hands that seemed to cling before releasing, she
was too far gone to know it. "Leah, no man can
live like we've been living without being tempted almost beyond endurance. I'm no saint, for
heaven's sake!"

"I thought my qualifications fell short of your
requirements," she flung at him, covering up
the agony of rejection with a show of disdain.

"Get yourself to bed, Leah. I'll apologize in the
morning."

"And you get yourself to the devil, Smith
Cairington!"

"Very likely," he replied wearily, closing the
door softly behind him.

Outside the moon that skirted the racing
clouds seemed to mock her through the open
window and she clenched her jaws until her
teeth hurt, determined not to give in to tears.

It might have been better had she cried it
out of her system. It would have relieved some
of the tension that pulled at her for the next
few days. As it was, she stiffened whenever she
heard his footsteps and tried to manage it so
that he had his meals alone on one pretext or
another.

"Oh, for crying out loud!" he exploded three
days later. He stood up from the table and flung
his napkin down and she could feel the heat of
his anger on her back as she chopped furiously
at the beef for mince. She had mumbled some-

thing about having to get it done before she had her own lunch, an empty excuse at best.

When he strode out to keep his daily radio appointment, she let her shoulders droop and then uttered a heartfelt curse as the knife slipped and nicked her between thumb and forefinger. She thought she had overcome her penchant for accidents!

The cut was not serious but it seemed inclined to bleed so she bundled up her hand in a towel and went in search of a plaster. It was when she was on her way back that she heard the crackle that preceded a transmission. Smith had slammed the door to the library with such force that it bounced open again and Leah stood outside with a certain amount of smug satisfaction and listened quite openly. While the act of eavesdropping would have shamed her, and rightly so, this seemed merely one for her in their constant game of one-upmanship.

Besides, he certainly couldn't be any more put out with her than he already was and if things got much worse, perhaps he'd take her back to the mainland and drop her off.

The thought that should have brought so much anticipation struck her with all the warmth of a January rain in Boston and she wondered how she could have undergone such a complete change of heart in a few short weeks without being aware of it.

"Chance there? Smith, this is Eve, come back."

Smith answered, his voice still showing traces

of his former burst of temper. "This is Chance, Eden, go ahead."

"There's a slight emergency on this end, Smith old dear."

"The emergency being that you've stood out in the sun too long without a hat, I take it," he came back sarcastically.

"Sorry, love, but the need for cover has gone, I'm afraid. The little parcel has been redirected and should be reaching you most any day now. Looks as if Eden's under your own feet now, old chum, and Adam's not going to reign in solitary splendor much longer. Ta ta."

"Hold it! Just a . . . look, in the clear, what's going on there?" Smith sounded fit to be tied and it did Leah an inordinate amount of good to know that she was not the only one out of favor at the moment.

"Not a thing at the moment. It all went on yesterday when someone let slip the fact that the *Sunfisher* had lain over in Rockhampton overnight before taking off to points unknown. Said parcel put two and two together and was as sweet as cane from then on. Suddenly decided to move on in search of fresh pastures, if you know what I mean. Nothing we can do at this end unless you'd like us to come along and dilute the mixture . . . in case it gets a bit sticky, that is."

Smith let out a string of profanity that didn't repeat itself from one end to the other and Leah moved closer to be certain his finger was not on the transmit button. There were laws, after all.

He glared at her balefully and she had the

grace to look ashamed at being caught listening
. . . not that she had tried to hide.

From an impossible low, his temper deterio-
rated even further and when she put the mince
on the table with a bowl of perfectly done
lyonnaise potatoes, he merely waded through
them as if they were so much wet sand. No
tender solicitation now for her various cuts and
bruises; he looked up from her newest plaster to
her face with a mocking expression and she
could hear the words as clearly as if he had
spoken them aloud, reminding her of her total
incompetence.

She was sorely tempted to quit. It wasn't as if
he were paying her wages for her long hours.
Well, not really long hours, but all the same, it
hadn't been easy. It would serve him right if she
refused to turn her hand to one more chore.

The more she thought of it, the better she liked
the idea. If he got angry enough he could only
take her back where he found her and the *Reef
Runner* would be long gone by now. She could
find herself a job in a restaurant, perhaps . . .
she might even try the pub where she first had
the misfortune to lay eyes on Smith Cairington.

She began her campaign the very next morning by not preparing breakfast. Smith said nothing. He simply rummaged in the pantry for
several minutes while she remained in her room
and by the time she emerged, he had gone about
his business. Filling her pockets with apples,
she slung an old windbreaker over her shoulders
and set out to explore the only part of the island
she had never visited, the east coast.

It was still cool with the clear light of morning sparkling on each blade of grass, but before long the sun would bake down on her shoulders, turning the areas beneath the trees into black caverns. She turned off on the unexplored bush track with a swinging stride and wondered if he had noticed her absence yet.

Tossing away one of the apple cores, she wished she had thought to bring a bite of cheese. A bit of protein never came amiss and breakfast had been a swallow of milk on her way out.

There was a patch of gorse and then the ground sloped down to a low, marshy aspect as she neared the shore. Birds of all sorts wheeled low overhead, squawking their outrage at being disturbed and she inhaled the not unpleasant scent of sun-baked mud and decaying vegetation.

There was an island of sorts just out a ways, a low, rocky nothing of an island that was connected to Chance by a hop-scotchy trail of rocks. It was an open dare and she barely hesitated before measuring the distance and making the first leap.

Child's play. She stopped halfway out and admired the luxurious growth of waving sea lettuce and something red and branchy that offered haven to a school of tiny, colorful fish, then moved on to her goal. The last jump was the broadest and she landed on the very edge of the water, her sneakers sinking up in wet sand over their tops. There was really very little sand at all, mostly sun-bleached coral rock with an occasional bit of greenery where some chance-dropped seed had taken root against all odds. No more than twenty feet long and half that across, it nevertheless gave her an exhilarating feeling of accomplishment and she stared out to where, if she remembered her geography, New Zealand should be rising up out of the Tasmin some thirteen hundred miles or so away.

"I proclaim you Leahland!" she called out to a jaded audience of gulls and gannets. She dropped the jacket and slipped off her shoes, rinsing them in the edge of the water and propping them out to dry. She had no intention of getting herself blistered by sandy wet shoes again! She stretched out on the windbreaker and gazed up at the clear sky, admiring the subtle shadings that ran the gamut from pink to robin's egg blue to cobalt directly overhead.

After awhile she began to wonder what Smith was doing at this moment. Had he missed her? No, he probably wouldn't even give her a thought until his stomach began to protest. She held up a slender leg and let her loose legged jeans fall back as she admired a delicate ankle. Her tan was something else again. If Iris could see her now, she'd sizzle with envy. They used to discuss the glamorizing effects of a good off-season tan back at school after lights out. What silly dreams they had indulged in back then.

Her mind drifted off and she must have dozed. The bolder of the birds had begun to take her presence for granted by now and stalked stiffly back and forth along the edges of the water, heads tilted to peer through the shallows in search of a morsel. She closed her eyes against the relentless sun and when she opened them again it was to find the sun covered with a gauzy veil of lightest gold.

She stretched her arms over her head stiffly and sat up, yawning openly. Water, water everywhere and not a drop . . . she was thirsty! It was at least an hour's walk back to the house but perhaps she could detour past the waterfall pool. The very thought made her mouth water and she picked up the jacket and looked around for the first rock stepping stone.

With a muzzy-headed blink, she turned in another direction, and then, fighting a growing panic, still another. The steps were not there. Not a single rock broke the silky surface of the water and with the sinking sun at that blindingly low angle, it was impossible to see below the surface. They might be two inches, they might be ten feet down.

"No, not ten feet, silly. The island is still high and dry." She spoke aloud in a forced cheerful voice but even as the words fell from her lips she saw that her island had shrunk to alarming proportions. Leahland was barely more than eight by twelve and the tide was lapping greedily at the edges, devouring the very rocks she had slept on moments ago.

Chapter Seven

The idea of swimming for it brought a shudder as she recalled tales she had heard from Bryce and Toby as well as from Smith, himself. Live coral cuts that gradually poisoned one's system, the sea urchins and sharks, morays and stingrays, barracuda and heaven knows what else that hovered stealthily beneath the deceptively lovely surface of these tropical waters.

Suddenly the cold gray waters of the Atlantic seemed so relatively harmless compared to exotic seas that hid a multitude of evils and she shivered and looked around for her shoes. They were nowhere to be found and then she remembered that the sunny spot where she turned them up to dry had been closer to the edge than the middle. They had floated away and now she was stranded here, barefooted and thirsty and unwilling to acknowledge, even to herself, just how close she was to the razor edge of panic.

The sun dropped behind the crest of Chance, bringing about an abrupt chill that made her huddle into the jacket for warmth. She watched the level of the tide apprehensively, wondering how soon it would cover the whole island. Leahland. That was a laugh! Leah lost . . . Leah's last stand, Leah . . . stop it!

Her mind was running around in circles, playing stupid word games in an attempt to avoid facing reality. It seemed she had some fatal flaw in her makeup that made it almost impossible for her to face unpleasant facts. She turned to the island that loomed so unreachably near. Chance. "Leah's last chance," she whispered with an unnerving tendency to giggle, and even through the sound of her own words, she heard an echo.

The echo of a whisper? Stop being so melodramatic, Leah Deerfield, she ordered herself, speaking aloud just to hear the sound of a human voice. It was growing steadily darker and she knew from experience that out here on the island it would grow very dark indeed before the sky would come alive with stars.

Again came the faint imaginary echo and she took a deep breath and looked up, waiting for the first stars to come into being.

"Leah, answer me! Leah!"

That was no echo!

"Smith? Smith, I'm out here!" she screamed, jumping up to stare into the darkness. There was nothing to see against the shadowy land-mass that seemed to float on a mirror of silvery water but she stared in the direction of the voice as if to bridge the space. "Smith? Please, I'm stranded!"

"Oh, my . . . you little fool, what are you doing out there? Wait, don't do anything!"

She hadn't been about to but she didn't say so. "I'm waiting."

"Well, give me a minute." He sounded thor-oughly out of sorts and she was suddenly ashamed of her childish behavior in running off without leaving a note. Here she was, trying to impress him with her maturity and she had to go and pull a stupid stunt like this!

"Got it," he said quietly. It was relatively silent at the moment but just a little while ago, the birds had been clamoring an unearthly din. "All right, Leah, you're going to sit down and relax while I talk, so find a comfortable spot and stay put." His voice sounded so calm and au-thoritative that she obeyed in spite of the rem-nants of her near panic. It was pride, she supposed, as well as her negligible amount of common sense that made her do as he asked with no demur. Not that she had much choice.

"I'm down but I can barely see," she told him, her voice only slightly unsteady.

"Good. Now, the tide turned about forty-five minutes ago and it's fairly swift around here so we'll just have to sit tight and be patient while it finishes off the job, right?"

"Smith, no!" she screamed, leaping to her feet. "Please don't leave me here! I'll do whatever you say; I'll go away if you want me to, but please don't leave me here to drown!" She broke off with a sob, finishing her plea on a broken note. "Please, Smith, I never meant to make you so angry."

"Leah!" It seemed that he had been calling her name for an endless time but through her sobs she could be sure of nothing.

Then there was a splash that registered dimly on her consciousness and she cringed, almost out of her head with fear.

"Leah, Leah, listen to me!" He sounded so close . . . her mind was playing tricks on her. She curled up into a small ball and covered her face, waiting to feel the first cold reaches of the tide that would engulf the island and her with it.

The cold came from overhead and rough hands dragged her to her feet. "Stop it!" he snarled, shaking her limp body. She grabbed at him, feeling solid, warm flesh beneath the clammy clothes and her tears turned to laughter that threatened to get out of control.

He rocked her as his hand connected with her cheek in a stinging blow but before she could utter a protest he had pulled her hard against his chest and was swaying with her, crooning to her almost as if she were a baby. "There, sweet, you didn't really think I was such a monster, did you? Stop crying, love, I'm here now and I'll

have you off this blasted rock in a minute or so."
More words rolled over her head and she took in
only their timbre, not their meaning. She
clutched him closer than close, as if she wanted
to crawl inside him and hide.

Smith finally succeeded in prying her arms
from around his neck and having her cling to his
back instead of his front. He clasped her behind
the knees and stood, shrugging her into a more
comfortable position, then he started off. It
was not until several minutes later that Leah
peered over her shoulder and saw, silhouetted
behind them against the rising moon, the same
knobby stepping stones breaking from a silvery
surface. She began to squirm, protesting that
they had definitely not been there before, but
Smith only shifted her weight and told her to
shut up and settle down.

She shut and settled. There was unbelievable
comfort in the warm solidity of his body beneath
hers; all the same, being carried piggyback over
rough terrain was not conducive to conversation, on the part of either participant. It was not
until they crested the rise that he sank down on
cool, bedewed grass and allowed her an explanation.

"You must have wandered out there just before the tide peaked. It began to drop within the
hour."

"Oh." The sound was almost too soft to be
heard.

"I was pretty sure those rocks would be breaking the surface if you'd only been in any shape to

wait," he told her. "You'd got yourself into a pretty fair state by then, though, and I couldn't calm you down from here."

"Weren't you afraid . . . swimming, I mean?"

"It's not exactly my favorite thing, plunging in where I can't see too well, but it's not the first time I've done it, by any means."

"I just want you to know how much I appreciate it . . . even if I don't really deserve it." She was recovering her equilibrium somewhat by now, but she still felt all hollow inside . . . as well as the worst kind of fool.

After awhile he asked her what had happened to her shoes and for some reason, a silly nursery rhyme popped into her head. "Bobby Shafto's gone to sea," she quoted brightly.

"Silver buckles and all," he finished drolly. "All right, waif, up and at 'em again." He stood and reached for her hand, pulling her protestingly to her feet beside him and leaning his back down.

"I can walk," she pointed out.

"Hang on," he ordered, ignoring her words as he leaned over and caught her legs.

The downhill going was easier although it jolted her with every step. She hated to think how Smith must be feeling with her flopping about on his back like a sack of flour. At least she wasn't cold anymore. Despite the fact that his clothes were wet and had quickly dampened her own, the heat that radiated from the contact between their two bodies was more than enough to offset the coolness of the night.

They entered through the back door and when he slid her to the floor, her knees almost buckled beneath her. She went first to the sink and drank her fill from the faucet and then she just hung there, her body cramped into the doubled over position it had taken for the past hour.

"Come on, honey," he urged gently, sounding as tired as she felt. And no wonder, she thought with a wash of guilt.

She attempted to apologize and it got all mixed up in her thanks but he shut her up with a short word and led her off down the hall. Her feet were dragging and when he paused outside her door to ask if she could make it, she shook her head in the negative.

With a sigh of resignation he shoved open her door and pushed her toward the bed. When she flopped across it, more asleep than awake, he grunted impatiently, fumbled at her waistband and tugged at her pantslegs and she felt her jeans sliding over her hips. Next came her shirt, with the buttons tangling painfully in her hair.

Smith paid no attention to her small protests; he was silent and she was only dimly aware of movement, then he fell down beside her, one arm flung carelessly across her bare back, and she thought he was asleep before his head hit the pillow.

Sometime during the night he must have covered them up with the light spread, and she vaguely remembered rousing once at the sound of a peculiar buzzing noise, but finding herself comfortably snuggled against his body, she drifted back into oblivion. He made a soft sound deep in his throat and settled her more comfortably against him, all without ever opening his eyes.

The next thing she heard was the sound of a door slamming. It might have been minutes later, or hours for all she knew, but she sat up and blinked through a curtain of hair when the door to her own room was flung open and someone spoke in loud, angry tones.

"Well, I figured there must be a reason for your little disappearing act, darling, but I didn't expect anything like this! Are congratulations in order?"

By this time both Leah and Smith were uncomfortably awake but before either of them could speak, the striking blond leaning against the doorjamb continued, her voice a strange, hard mixture of amusement and anger. "No, I'm sure your dear sister would have been only too delighted to tip me off if that had been the case, so I can only suppose you've been up to a bit of discreet tomcatting."

"Have the grace to disappear for a little while, Helen," Smith said in a voice that struck Leah as infinitely weary.

Instead, the woman strolled over to the side of the bed and leaned over to pick something off the floor. "My, my, we were in a hurry, weren't we, love? Perhaps I stayed away too long after all." She uttered a laugh that held nothing of humor as she extended his crumpled khakis to him. "Shall I fetch a wrap for your little doxy? It would be tearose satin with acres of lace, I suppose . . . or perhaps poison pink chiffon with marabou? Dreadfully passé, but then I always did adore bad movies and this has all the earmarks."

"Just shut up, Helen. You've had your fun so get out or be thrown out!"

"My, my, aren't we the big, tough hero? Sounds as if you might have missed out on your own fun, but then you should pay more attention to the selection of leading ladies, darling. You're slipping," Helen sang softly as she closed the door with a mocking smirk.

When Helen had entered the room, Leah had fallen back to the pillow numbly, dragging the covers up under her chin. The numbness was beginning to wear off by now and she fought to bring it back. "Who . . . ?"

"Sorry about that, Leah. Helen's inclined to be a bit of a pain at times." He didn't even glance at her as he slid out of bed and for that she was eternally grateful; she couldn't have possibly hidden the way she felt at that moment and it would only give him another whip with which to flog her.

He stepped into his wrinkled pants and fastened the belt, ignoring the shirt that was caught up on the bedpost. "Take your time," he offered tersely, striding from the room in a manner that boded ill for someone.

If Leah thought the day could go nowhere but uphill from that low point, she soon discovered her mistake. A formal introduction to Helen Craddock, daughter of one of the higher management of Cairington Enterprises, in no way put an end to the sniping. Some of it was blatant enough to bring a thunderous look to Smith's face but after he ordered the older girl to either behave herself or get off the island, it became more subtle.

"Looks as if I have no choice, love," Helen drawled, allowing a smoke ring to drift from her perfectly made up mouth. "I came by air-taxi and naturally I couldn't leave the poor man waiting with the meter ticking away. 'Fraid you'll just have to put up with me."

Lunch was a painful affair and Leah, due primarily to pure nerves, managed to overbake the meat and overseason the vegetables. The fact that no one commented on her lamentable failure made it even worse and she was in a distinctly sour mood by the time the last dish was washed.

It seemed that Helen was anxious to make the most of her visit and she prevailed on Smith to take her waterskiing after lunch. It was a sport Leah had never even attempted, much less mastered, and so she found herself left to her own devices.

The small bedroom was on the side of the house that caught the first rays of the morning sun. It did not have its own bath and lacked storage space as well and Leah, entering with fresh sheets, eyed the two suitcases Helen had left outside the door with disquiet. The other girl was certainly no stranger to the island and she was a close friend of Smith's as well, probably much more than a close friend, if the truth were known.

So who rated the second best bedroom, a girlfriend of long-standing who turned up unexpectedly or a stowaway, known to no one, who had been promoted grudgingly to chief cook and bottle washer?

By late afternoon, Leah had switched rooms and was in the kitchen trying to decide on a foolproof dinner menu when Smith and Helen came in, laughing over something Helen had said when they paused outside the door. Smith dropped a string of fish on the drainboard and Helen, her cheeks glowing under her golden tan, pronounced herself starving.

"I was just trying to decide what to have," Leah told her.

"Oh, don't bother. Smith and I caught half a dozen tailers in no time at all, so we'll grill them on the patio. I'll do my special salad and we'll have crisps from a tin. Roughing it, hmm, darling? Remember the oven fries I made that time we got caught up at the outstation?"

For the next few days, Leah found herself demoted from cook to helper and it was not a particularly welcome event, oddly enough. Helen, as well as her skill at all water sports and Lord knows what else, was a first rate cook and delighted in producing meals of a cordon bleu class. It was left to Leah to tackle the mountain of utensils used in the preparation of such feasts. The change in rooms went unnoticed, or at least, it wasn't mentioned.

Leah had a quiet moment of amusement picturing Smith's face if he came to what he thought was Helen's room for a romantic session and found, instead, only Leah. The amusement had a strangely bitter taste, though, and she began inventing excuses not to accompany them on various expeditions. She neither skied, nor dived and so she found herself left to weed the garden or tackle the washing while the other two stayed busy from morning till night.

"Stop feeling sorry for yourself, you little ninny," she scolded one morning as she scoured the grill and banged it down on the counter. "It's still room and board and half the work's been taken over, at that!"

Smith came in and glanced at her with surprise. "Still at it?"

"Well, what did you expect? Steaks, plus omelets, plus stewed fruit, plus muffins, plus . . ."

"All right, all right, point taken. Helen has a lavish hand when it comes to fixing a man's breakfast."

"Then you might say," Leah returned sarcastically, "that I have a lavish hand when it comes to cleaning up after a man's breakfast."

He turned toward her, eyes narrowed and head tilted quizzically. "I get the impression you don't exactly approve of Helen."

"Approve? Why should I approve or disapprove?" she exclaimed a little wildly. "Your guests have nothing whatsoever to do with me!"

Before she could put down the pan she was drying with a determination that threatened the finish, he was in front of her, standing disturbingly close. His hands closed over her shoulders and slipped down her arms to catch her hands. Impatiently, he removed the pan and then placed both her hands over his shoulders to grin down at her. "If you weren't such a baby, I'd say you were jealous," he ventured with infuriating satisfaction.

"Jealous! Of Helen? Ha!"

"Oh, our Helen's not to be taken lightly, now. Hasn't she told you she's the area tennis champ, she's won most of the women's events at race meets for the past half a dozen years, and can hold her own at master's bridge tournaments, as well?"

"How nice to be Helen!" Leah retorted, torn between wanting to wipe that provocative grin right off his face and wanting to bury her face in his warm, brown throat, revealed so tantalizingly by the open neck of his soft, blue corduroy shirt.

"Somebody take my name in vain?" Helen sang out, letting the door swing noisily closed behind her. "Hanky-panky with the hired help, darling? I thought you were fetching us a beer." She turned to Leah and the lightness of her tone was nowhere in evidence in the pale, mascaraed eyes. "We're going surf fishing out from the coral pool. Don't wait lunch for us, okay?"

"Better yet," Smith interposed, "come with us. There's no reason you can't throw in a line . . . the fish don't know the difference from their end."

"Smith," Helen began, but he ignored her and took the dish towel from Leah's hands and turned her in the direction of her room.

"Get on a bathing suit and a wrap. Wear your tennis shoes, too. This time, we'll keep 'em dry." He swatted her familiarly on her bottom and Leah could just imagine Helen's mood at the thought of their twosome being enlarged. It was the deciding factor.

"My sneakers . . . remember?" she prompted from the door.

"Bobby Shafto. Something else then . . . surely you have something flat that will do to scramble out on the reef in? Maybe Helen could lend you something . . . on second thought, you'd be lost in her shoes."

Leah left them and returned a few minutes later wearing cut off jeans, sweat shirt and a pair of crepe soled flats that she consigned to ruin. Salt would leave a white ring that was inerasable but not for any such trivial matter would she miss the outing.

Smith carried the rods and tackle, Leah was handed a small cooler and a bucket that smelled to high heaven and Helen walked between them, her beautifully manicured hands empty.

It was a matter of bafflement to Leah how the older girl, who spent her days fishing, diving or skiing and then managed to prepare scrumptious meals each evening could look so band-box perfect on all occasions. She wore white

invariably . . . brief shorts and a briefer halter,
silk lounging pajamas, a minuscule bikini that
brought a flush to Leah's cheeks the first time
she had seen it. There was so *much* of her, and it
was all so perfectly proportioned, so exquisitely
groomed and beautifully dressed . . . or un-
dressed. How could anyone compete with a
goddess who could do everything better than
any mere mortal, with half the effort?

But who said anything about competing?
Leah derided herself as she trotted along behind
the other two, her nose averted from the smelly
bait bucket. She amused herself by watching the
long, voluptuous legs flashing before her and
wondering how long before all that lush perfec-
tion softened into middle-aged spread. Helen
must be almost as old as Smith and he was
somewhere in his mid-thirties . . . old enough to
consider Leah herself, a mere child. The
thought rankled anew and she reminded herself
that there had been a few occasions when he
had been under no such misapprehension . . .
although he seemed happy enough for the past
few days to relegate her to the ranks of those to
be neither seen nor heard.

"Tide's about right now, so we'll try for a few
tailers off the outer ring, all right?" Smith
suggested as he rammed three rod holders into
the sand.

Fishing, as far as Leah was concerned, was a
thing done with a cork and a cane pole, a sport
that bore little resemblance to whipping hun-
dreds of dollars worth of fiberglass and chrome

over one's shoulder to send an all but invisible line miles out to sea. With Smith's instruction, she finally managed to get her baited hook a few yards out from the low-lying reef where they were located.

Helen had taken a promontory off to the left as her own, sending her artificial lure in a beautiful long arc, only to reel it in and send it out again. Smith's patience seemed unending as he instructed Leah in the fine art of spin casting and for some reason, that very patience seemed to irritate Helen no end.

"For heaven's sake, Smith, put it out there for her and let her hold the darn thing. She won't catch anything, anyway," Helen snapped from her vantage point, looking like some modern-day figurehead, all golden tan and proud in her tiny white bikini.

Disdaining to answer, he merely showed Leah again the proper way to cast without tripping the line too soon.

"Why couldn't I just use yours?" Leah asked finally in desperation. He had given the two girls the shiny, sleek spincasting rods and kept for his own use a battered looking bamboo with a simple level wind reel.

"Because knowing you, you'd end up with a blistered thumb and the granddaddy of all backlashes. This one is simpler once you master it, so look smart and we'll try again." He reached around her to demonstrate the proper hold and she was far more conscious of his body touching her back than the skill he was demonstrating.

That had been the trouble all along, she acknowledged dolefully. For days now, ever since Helen's untimely arrival, Leah had drawn herself up into a tight little knot, refusing to feel, refusing even to think about the fact that her unlikely idyll had ended. Ended just in time, too, she chided herself, for she had been drifting along with the idea that Smith was coming to care for her just a little. That was a laugh! With a girl friend like Helen waiting in the wings, he must have been simply bored stiff to have allowed himself to notice someone like herself, even for a minute!

"Smith!" she exclaimed, suddenly jarred out of her dismal thoughts, "someone's tugging on my line!"

"Well, reel him in, you nitwit!" Smith laughed, stepping back to allow her room.

Almost choking in her excitement, she landed a lively three pounder and could hardly wait to get her line rebaited and back in the water.

The next two were caught by Helen, who had watched Leah's triumph with a slight sneer. They were both slightly larger than Leah's but that in no way lessened the younger girl's enjoyment and she was disappointed when Smith announced it was time to quit, as the tide had turned.

"Besides, this sun will fool you out here on the water. No point in risking trouble. I'll stow the gear and then we'll take a dip, all right?"

With her eyes on the tall figure skipping agilely across the rocks toward the shore with his burden, Leah slowly shucked off her jeans and shirt.

"Just how long have you two known each other, anyway?" Helen asked from behind her. She had approached silently and now stood, as did Leah, watching Smith ram the rods in their holders and put the fish on ice.

"What? Oh . . . not all that long, really," Leah stalled. She had no idea what Smith had told his friend about her, but there had been no questions up until now.

"Smith said something about knowing your father in New York and running into you again in Rockhampton. Lucky for *some* people, I must say!"

"Oh . . . well, yes, it was. I've enjoyed my . . . holiday here," Leah said weakly.

"Well, enjoy it while you can, because once we get back to the mainland, there'll be no more fun and games . . . at least not unless I'm the partner. He told me he was working all those nights in New York when he couldn't come to dinner or theater, but it looks as if I let him slip the leash, doesn't it? But then, we'll call it a bachelor's last fling, shall we? I believe it's traditional."

Before Leah could come up with a reply, Helen brushed past her and dived over, scarcely rippling the surface so sleekly did she enter the water. She did a slow roll, then came up to float on the surface and while Leah was staring absently at the wavering shadow on the sand below her, Smith spoke from behind her. Really, she was becoming so absentminded these days a herd of elephants would have to trumpet twice to get her attention!

"We've been remiss in not swimming here lately."

She glanced up in time to catch the significant gleam in his eyes and felt the slow color stain her face. He was reminding her none too subtly of the only other time she had visited the pool! Refusing to rise to his provocation, she dived swiftly in and came up swimming.

It was on the way back to the house that Smith announced plans to leave the following morning. Helen seemed not to care, either way, but Leah was stunned by her own reaction. Was she such a masochist that she'd rather remain here with the two of them than part from Smith for good? Because that's what it would mean. Once they reached the mainland again, there'd be no reason to prolong the relationship further. He'd simply drop her off and go on back to Melbourne with Helen. From the hints the other girl had dropped and her easy familiarity with the various members of the Cairington family, there'd be an engagement announcement before long and she had no intention of being within a thousand miles when that happened.

It was after Leah had gone to her room to pack that Helen looked in on her. She closed the door quietly behind her and crossed to where Leah's three suitcases were opened on the bed.

"Hmmm, ready for the siege, aren't you?" she asked, fingering a raw silk print that had never even been worn. "One wouldn't think from the way you've dressed since I've been here that you knew one designer from another but I recognize this one . . . she's a bit fussy for my tastes, but I understand she's fairly popular with the upwardly mobile classes."

"Are you cooking dinner tonight or am I?" Leah asked grimly, refusing to rise to the bait.

"Oh, I'll do the roast . . . after all, I know just how Smith likes it. What I wanted to say, darling, is that it would be better to make a clean break of it once we reach Rockhampton. I mean, you could make things sticky and embarrassing but I'm sure you wouldn't want to, for Smith's sake. Men hate that sort of thing, don't they?"

Leah swallowed her indignation and nodded her head. Speech was beyond her at the moment.

"I was going to offer you . . . well, you never know, I mean, you might have needed the kitty fattened up a bit, but I see that you're all right as far as that goes. Smith would have taken care of that, himself, no doubt, but I thought you'd rather have it just between us girls." She smiled sweetly with her glistening rose-gold mouth, while the pale gray-blue eyes passed on a warning that was unmistakable and Leah simply returned to her packing, slamming closed the drawer that had held her underwear.

By the time she came out to set the table for dinner, there were still flags flying in her eyes, but she answered politely when Helen mentioned using the china instead of the ironstone. She ran into Smith as she crossed the dining

room. He had entered from the hall doorway
and had caught her arms and looked down
with a quizzical gleam. "Hey, slow down there,
where's the parade?" He looked behind her to
where the baize door between kitchen and dining room still swung on its silent hinges and
lifted an eyebrow. "Come on into the library for
a minute, will you?"

Without waiting for her acquiescence, he pro-
pelled her forward and not until they were inside
the book-lined room did he speak again. "Did
Helen say anything to upset you?" he asked
intently.

"Why should you think that?" she shrugged,
her eyes avoiding him.

"Because after all this time, I think I know
you pretty well, little Leah, and something's got
your dander up. Since it wasn't my doing this
time, I can only assume it was Helen."

When she didn't answer, didn't raise her face
to return his searching gaze, he continued;
"Look, honey, I've known Helen all my life and
while she's a great gal in a lot of ways, she can
be pretty outspoken when it suits her. Just don't
take anything she said too seriously, will you?"

"Why should I? It's certainly nothing to me,
and besides . . . well, anyone as beautiful and as
talented as Helen can afford to be outspoken,
can't they?" With all her heart she longed to
hear him say that Helen wasn't all *that* talented,
and wasn't *really* so beautiful.

He grinned broadly, shaking his head. "I'll
have to admit there's little she can't tackle

and polish off first class, through sheer determination, if nothing else. The woman's got a
drive to succeed that would probably land her
a seat in parliament if she turned her aristocrat-
ic nose in that direction."

None of which made Leah feel any more
charitable when she returned to her task of
laying the table. Helen had changed into a white
silk dinner gown that was slit up to her thigh
and this time she had opted for a splash of color
in the scarlet poppies that trailed down one side.

"Put some fresh candles in the candelabra,
will you? I fancy the red . . . they're in the
right-hand drawer. We need a festive touch
tonight since it's in way of a last night celebration." Helen placed the five-branched Georgian
silver piece on the table and called out to Smith
to open the wine and allow it to breathe.

The table done, Leah returned to her room and
stripped off her jeans and shirt. She had showered on returning from the coral pool and her
hair was soft and silky, tied back with its scarf,
but tonight that wasn't enough. It might be the
last dinner she'd have with Smith and she may
as well leave him a mental picture in case he
ever spared her a thought after dropping her off
at Rockhampton.

A few minutes later she suffered Helen's
derisive glance as she entered the dining room
in her soft, creamy, wool crepe. The dress had
shawl sleeves with a self-fringe and the low
cowled neckline was a perfect foil for the an-
tique necklace of cairngorm that matched her

hair. The hair, itself, was done in a loose bundle held back from her face with invisible clips and she felt slightly more able to hold her own wearing three-inch heels.

After that one sharp glance, Helen turned her attention to the man who was pouring the wine. "I got out the burgundy, Smith. What happened?"

"Nothing, my dear. I simply thought the cabernet a better choice," he replied blandly, lifting his eyes from the stemmed glass to give Leah a warm, appreciative look. She was grateful for his forbearance in not mentioning her unaccustomed finery; it would have been even more embarrassing to have a big thing made of it.

The table looked lovely and Helen's standing rib roast was a masterpiece, complete with braised potatoes and *petit pois*. As for the candelabra, Leah soon discovered that there was a very effective use for a tall candelabra on a table set for three. Smith was seated in his usual place at the head of the table with Helen on his right and Leah at the other end, well hidden behind the gleaming centerpiece.

The conversation was immediately taken over by Helen and maintained almost nonstop while Smith served the succulent pink beef and the perfectly done vegetables. Leah sat silent, her unfocused eyes staring at the bright points of light while she listened to the other girl rattle on about James, who was finishing up as a jackeroo on a station in South Australia and Mickey, who

was in Mt. Isa learning the ropes in order to take
his place with the family mining interest.

"What do you think of the beef, darling? Too
rare?" she put in after a monologue on the
coming social events in Melbourne.

"The beef's perfect," Smith said firmly. "I
wish I could say as much for the table setting."

"Oh, darling, don't embarrass the poor girl.
She did her very best and a little ostentation is
understandable at that age, don't you agree? I
think it looks very nice," she finished sanctimo-
niously.

"If you'll excuse me, I think I've had enough,"
Leah choked. She pushed back her chair and
gathered up her silver, stifling the urge to throw
it at the two who remained at the table.

"Oh, but your dessert!" Helen cried, distress
touching her perfect features lightly. "I've done
a perfectly lovely pavlova and you know you
won't want to miss that. I thought all youngsters
loved sweets."

"None for me, thanks, but I'll be glad to serve
yours," Leah told her with grim amusement as
she stalked out to the kitchen. If she had to stay
and listen to one more word in those cultured,
dulcet tones, she'd explode, standing rib, *petit
pois*, potatoes and all!

The dessert plates were ready beside the
picture-perfect confection and Leah, the begin-
nings of a thin smile on her face, cut an enormous slice for Smith and a slightly more modest
one for Helen. There was evidently one thing his
lady love didn't know about Smith Cairington,
she thought with a delicious surge of malice,

and she'd stand there and watch him down the last morsel if it choked him!

By the time the sun broke over the low-lying cloud bank the next morning, the tanks had been topped off, the perishable food packed in the coolers for snacking along the way and Leah had stripped the beds and remade them with fresh linen. She had noted with uncharitable satisfaction Helen's pale, shaky looks over a tomato juice and black coffee breakfast and thought the older girl had probably stayed up to do a little extra celebrating after she, herself, had retired. She had done her share of demolishing the dinner wine, even if it had not been her own choice, Leah remembered, and then she went on to recall the scene at the table when Smith had eyed the generous serving of dessert, cast a withering look at Leah and announced in no uncertain terms what he thought of such sickening concoctions.

He had probably been called upon to placate the shattered Helen, Leah decided on seeing his own slightly grim face on his way down to the *Sunfisher* with the first load of luggage. Well, it served them both right, Smith for going along with a joke long after he should have ended it and Helen . . . well, just for being Helen!

On the way to the jetty, she turned for one last look at the place where, unexpectedly, she had been happier than any other place. She fought down a ridiculous desire to cry her eyes out and blinked before continuing on down the path.

"All right, honey?" Smith asked quietly, coming up behind her.

His voice brought a steadying effect to her wobbling chin and she turned to smile blindingly at him. "I've learned a lot, believe it or not. Thanks for your patience . . . on occasion."

"So've I, little one, so have I. It hasn't been a bad exercise for either one of us, come to that."

The trip back to the mainland was far more comfortable than the run out, especially remembering the hot, airless cabin where she had hidden away. Now she sat up on the cabin, braced against the flying bridge and left the other two to each other's company. Not that there was much chance for conversation, for Smith seemed determined to run flat out and the noise was terrific.

Not only the noise, she realized with chagrin an hour or so after they got underway; the motion of the dead-rise hull spanking over a choppy sea was beginning to have a peculiar effect on her insides and she made her way ignominiously below.

By the time Smith came down to check up on her she was too miserable to do more than groan at him to go away.

"If I'd thought about it, honey, I'd have dosed you up before we left Chance. I'm afraid it's too late now."

"It's too late for anything, so please, will you just get out?" she agonized, feeling greener by the minute.

He squeezed her shoulder in commiseration then left, and she only hoped he wouldn't send Helen down to minister to her. That would be the final indignity!

When she came up again, after dozing fitfully, she was amazed to see the modest skyline of Rockhampton moving smoothly alongside. Smith cut the throttle and eased in beside a sports cruiser displaying flags to indicate two black marlin and Leah turned and retraced her steps to gather up her luggage. It was too soon! She felt like hiding out in the forward cabin again and waiting for a magic trip back in time, but it was no good. She had shied away from facing facts in the past; there was no choice now.

Bags lined up alongside the harbor half an hour later, Helen turned to Leah while Smith spoke to the dock guard and said, "Where shall we drop you? I imagine Smith and I will head for the airport. We can be home before dinner time if the winds hold in this direction."

Floundering wildly, Leah tried to think of a likely place to be set down. "Well . . . I guess you could drop me at a bus station," she said finally.

"Good enough. Here, Smith's commandeered a cab."

They were herded in, with the two women in the back seat and Smith in front beside the driver and Helen leaned forward and said something to Smith as they wheeled away from the waterfront.

Rockhampton was not all that large a town and it was several minutes before it occurred to Leah that the coach station must be an unlikely distance away. Just as she leaned forward to speak, Helen forestalled her.

"Smith, I *said* Leah wants to go to the bus station. She has her plans made and I promised we'd drop her off."

By this time, they were turning into what was unmistakably an airport and Helen bit off her plea with an unladylike oath. The cab pulled up with a nice bit of showmanship and the two men got out and began hauling bags from the trunk while Helen fumed and Leah stared helplessly into the peach and gold colored sunset. The warm light that covered everything lent a certain air of unreality and when she saw a familiar looking couple approaching them, she didn't even give them a second look.

"There's Eve," Helen remarked. "They must have just landed."

Before Leah could react, Smith had taken her elbow and was propelling her into a sleek looking machine with the modest insignia of a Beechcraft Baron. "Stay put, will you? I'll explain later."

She watched through the perspex while the four on the ground converged, Helen gesticulating angrily to Smith and the couple from the *Sunfisher,* the couple she had seen a month ago, looking with perplexed expressions from the plane, where she herself sat, to the man and the girl beside him. In less than five minutes, Smith was urging Helen through the door and into the front seat beside him and before Leah could protest, they were taxiing down the runway.

It was one thing to stow away; it was quite another to find herself shanghaied . . . or was it skyjacked?

"Stay buckled up, Leah. Might be a bit bumpy for the first hour," Smith said laconically over his shoulder.

She settled back in resignation and stared at the two relaxed forms in front of her. No doubt Helen was as good a flyer as she was everything else, but it was evident who the captain was and in this case, his word was law. Whatever Helen or she herself thought, Smith Cairington had his own ideas about her disposal.

God, what a race of supermen, she thought wryly. The older couple had obviously flown here in the Baron and would now swap for the *Sunfisher*. Helen had told her, not realizing that it was news, that Chance belonged to Cairington Enterprises and that Howard and Eve Blane had built the house after Howard had had to retire prematurely for health reasons.

Thoughts of the couple whom she now knew were Smith's older sister and brother-in-law could only bring back memories of the first time she had seen them. That they remembered her had been evident from their expressions in the few minutes before taking off. She wondered what on earth Smith had told them. For that matter, she wondered just what he had told Helen? One thing was certain; he went his own way without either consulting or explaining.

Totally drained from the long day as well as the past several restless nights, Leah slept to the lulling drone of the powerful engines. If there was any meaningful dialogue between the two up front, she missed it, rousing only in time to be bundled off and into a waiting car.

Chapter Eight

The sun shone on Melbourne, too, but it was not the same sun that had warmed Chance Island, Leah decided sadly. She had been here two days, an uneasy guest of an absentee host, and it had taken her some time to accept the fact that the man she had bickered with and cooked for on the island was a wealthy socialite whose business interests carried him to the other side of the world as easily as she would have taken a bus from school into town a few years ago.

Cairington Place was the equivalent of one of England's lesser stately homes. It had taken her aback to find herself led through tall ceilinged rooms across priceless Oriental carpets to a bedroom the likes of which she had only seen in films. Helen had complained about it the morning after they arrived, having gone almost immediately to her usual room. That fact had registered, too, no matter how tired Leah had been, the fact that Helen had a "usual room" in Smith's home.

The housekeeper, Mrs. Alden, had taken charge of her at Smith's behest, putting her in an enormous, pink carpeted room and then offering to unpack and run a bath for her. Leah had been too weary to even think about anything except that enormous, inviting, satin-covered bed, but she found herself being shunted from bedroom to bath and back to bed again almost as if she were a child.

She surfaced again when the sun was pouring through the windows to see Mrs. Alden bringing a tea tray and she sat up guiltily, protesting the special treatment.

"Mr. Cairington had to fly to Tokyo this morning, but he asked me to look after you and see that you had some pampering," the gray-haired woman informed her.

Sitting up in bed with a sinking feeling in her stomach, Leah took the tea gratefully but rejected any idea of pampering. "Did he say how long he was to be gone?" she asked as the older woman opened the brocaded draperies wider and closed the window.

"Oh, he'll be back day after tomorrow. Meanwhile, Miss Helen will show you around town. You've not seen Melbourne before, Mr. Cairington tells me."

"No," Leah allowed, struggling with the idea of sightseeing under the aegis of Helen Craddock. She had an idea that the idea appealed no more to Helen than it did to her, but there was no point in protesting to the housekeeper.

"Does . . . does Mr. Cairington live here all the time?" What a stupid question, she chided herself, but the other woman answered easily, "Oh, no, Miss Deerfield. He spends a good bit of time out at the homestead with his mother and then he has to make regular visits to the London office, too, but since Helen's father will be taking that over, he'll have even more time to spend here at home." Some of the fresh good humor seemed to evaporate from the woman's face and she made an excuse of having to see to Miss Helen's breakfast tray and left.

As things turned out, she needn't have worried about being too much in Helen's company; after a brief outburst about Leah's having been given the room usually reserved for Smith's mother, Helen subsided into a sulky silence and spent most of her time on the phone.

Unwilling to give Mrs. Alden anything to worry about, Leah took herself exploring by bus, a feat that first involved a walk of almost a quarter of a mile just to reach the street. She simply rode the route that first day, making note of what she wanted to see later on.

Smith came home just before dinnertime on the second day, gray with fatigue, and promptly disappeared into the room Leah had learned was his home office, sacrosanct even to Helen.

She wanted to speak to him about finding work

and a place to stay, for she felt very much the
intruder in spite of Mrs. Alden's kindly ministra-
tions, but he didn't emerge until long after she
had gone up to bed.

That was another thing; why had he instructed Mrs. Alden to put her in the pink room that
first night? Helen had gone ahead, merely ascer-
taining that she was to have her usual room, and
Smith had introduced Leah to the housekeeper
and charged the latter to see to her comfort and
have Homer put her bags in the pink room.

Oh, well, it looked as if she'd have to make the
move herself without waiting for Smith's ap-
proval. By the time she got downstairs the morning after his arrival, he had already left for
the offices downtown and Helen informed her
that the two of them were to do the town again.

"Again?" Leah blurted, in spite of herself.

"I didn't figure you were any more anxious for
my company than I was yours. Just what Smith
has in mind for you, I don't know. I suspect,
since he knows your father, it's a matter of
keeping the paternal eye on you until you get
your bearings, but there's a round of events
coming up in the next few weeks that Smith and
I always attend together and I'm sure you'll
want to be long gone by then. I mean, it can't be
much fun to be a fifth wheel, can it?"

They taxied into town and browsed the Royal
Arcade, where Helen bought three pairs of shoes
and a new white shantung suit. When she
announced that she had an appointment to have
her hair done, Leah was glad of a chance to take
off on her own, and with an agreement to make

their separate ways back to Cairington Place,
they split up.

Strolling along Collins Avenue, Leah watched
the bustle of trams and autos, the crowds of
people who all looked as if they had somewhere
to go and someone waiting for them when they
arrived. In an odd sort of way, she was homesick
for the States. There was no particular place
there that drew her, certainly not her father's
luxurious condominium that had been the nearest thing to a home she had.

It was the light; something about the angle of
the sun, the time of year, which brought back
memories, none of them particularly happy
ones, and she knew she was allowing herself to
drift aimlessly like the small wooden boat some
child had risked and lost on the Yarra River. She
remembered the child as he straightened up
from his precarious perch, reconciled himself to
his loss with a funny little shrug of his shoulders
and turned away. Why couldn't she be as ma-
ture? What was preventing her from turning her
back on her losses and breaking away from a
situation that could only end in pain and embarrassment for her? Smith only tolerated her from
some unlikely sense of responsibility and Helen
made no pretense of wanting her there. In the
near future, if Helen could be believed, and
Leah saw nothing to indicate otherwise, Helen
would be mistress of Cairington Place and certainly before that happened, Leah would have to
make her escape.

She got up from her bench and strolled along
the shady sidewalk, her eyes following the chil-

dren who were spilling out of the gates of one of
the city's many parks, but her thoughts still
turned inward. It was the caravan that slowed
down to turn into the park entrance that trig-
gered a chain of thought that brought her to a
standstill and then she turned and trotted along
after it until she could read the name on the
side. The word "Handicapped" had stood out in
her inattentive mind and now she made a note
of the full name: The Kincaid School For The
Handicapped.

All the way back to the Cairington home, she
wondered how to go about approaching them for
a job. She considered asking Smith for his help,
for it was entirely possible that he knew someone connected with the school. She didn't really
care what she did, knowing that every job in
such an establishment was important, for the
total environment was crucial to the successful
treatment of those special children.

Then she discarded the idea of asking for help.
If she were going to do this thing, she'd do it
alone. Maybe afterward, when she had a room
and a job of her own, she'd write him a note of
thanks for all he had done for her.

Thank him for what? she thought with unaccustomed bitterness, for allowing her to become
so completely under his spell that even now she
couldn't bear the thought of his future with
Helen, of the two of them spending vacations
alone on Chance Island?

The cab pulled up in front of the house just as
Smith was getting out of his own gunmetal
Jensen. Leah payed the man and added a more

generous tip than she could afford, hardly taking her eyes from the man who was coming to meet her, his hand in his pocket.

"You should have let me settle up, Leah," he accused gently as the cab rolled down the graveled driveway.

"There's no reason why you should," she countered easily, more easily than she felt as she mounted the bank of steps at his side. He looked unfairly handsome in a suit of some hard finish wool in a storm cloud gray. "You've done more than enough for me as it is, more than I can every repay."

He took her arm and tucked it under his own, even though they were almost at the door. "Let's have no such talk between us, girl. I'm sorry, by the way, that I had to dash off as soon as we arrived, but I hope Helen's been taking good care of you in my absence."

Since it was not a question, she did not feel compelled either to confirm or deny. At any rate, before she could do either, the door was thrown open and Helen confronted them.

"Smith, you're late! Did you forget that we were to go to the Worthington's for drinks? I promised Mitzi you wouldn't back out this time and they have that spelunker who spoke to the Adventurer's Club last year . . . what was his name, Theodore? Theodore something."

Leah went directly to her room, leaving Helen to follow Smith into the morning room, still chattering on about Theodore whatever and his spelunking safaris. If the two of them were going out tonight that meant she could have a tray in her room again. It also meant listening to the friendly, garrulous Mrs. Alden rattle on about the Cairington boys and their perpetual pranks and she'd just as soon not have any more reminders of them . . . or one of them, at least. For that matter, the room itself was a reminder, as was the house and the very city.

Let's face it, Leah, my girl, from now on, whatever you see or hear or do, you'll be reminded of Smith Cairington. Immediately, a vision of cool, gray eyes and dark, unruly hair swam before her eyes and she made an impatient sound. Perhaps she'd have better luck getting him out of her system once she was away from his immediate sphere. It would be better if she could go someplace else, but she lacked funds to get very far, and besides, there was the Kincaid School and she had a hunch about it. Seeing the van had been almost like an omen and she was never one to ignore the signs.

She luxuriated in a bath, reminding herself that it might be one of the last great baths she'd enjoy for some time to come. From now on it would be basic digs and she'd be lucky not to have to share.

After a delicious supper of broiled fish, she stretched out across her bed to plan her attack for the next morning. She could call, but that would give them the chance to say no. Better to go and face them; surely they'd find it harder to tell her to her face that there was no place for her there.

Her mind rambled from the shady streets of downtown Melbourne to a secluded freshwater pond with a tiny waterfall and then to a rocky island silhouetted against a silvery sea. When next she opened her eyes it was to see Smith standing over her.

"I knocked but there was no answer," he murmured. He seemed to be devouring her with his eyes and when she realized that she was wearing only the thin wrap she had put on after her bath, she pulled the blanket over her.

"What did you want?" she demanded.

"I wanted to talk to you. It seems we haven't had time for more than a word or two since we left the island."

"That's hardly my fault."

"No, I realize that." He sat down beside her and she moved her feet, afraid to come in physical contact with him.

"Scared of being burned?" he jeered softly. "You weren't that frightened on Chance." The cool mockery in his eyes was a painful reminder of those first days.

"Don't flatter yourself," she replied tightly, striving for composure. Here in the warm intimacy of the ultra-feminine room he seemed very large and dangerously masculine and she hated her own weakness for the thrill of excitement that ran through her. She resorted to flippancy; "You were the only man there and I was bored."

Smith threw back his head and laughed and she watched in fascination the play of muscles beneath the smooth, bronzed skin of his throat.

"Oh, so that's your story, is it?" He reached out lazily and captured her head, drawing her forward until, off balance, she toppled against him. "It won't wash, young Leah. I'll admit, I might have suspected something of the sort that first time we met but by the time we reached the island, I was beginning to have second thoughts. No, child, there's no way you can convince me you're anything but what you so obviously are," he murmured, rubbing his chin against her hair.

"And what's that?" she asked breathlessly, half afraid of his answer.

"Ah, that would be telling," he teased, "although it wouldn't take all that much right now to talk me into pretending."

"Pretending what?" she managed past the lump that had lodged somewhere in the vicinity of her throat.

"That you'd welcome this," he replied deeply, tipping her face up to meet his lips as he kissed her eyes, one after the other. "And this," he breathed against her lips. His mouth was cool and firm, as if he restrained himself forcibly, and with a small, choking sound, she responded in spite of all her fine resolves. Her arms came up around his neck and after a momentary hesitation he captured her mouth with a kiss that plundered her very soul.

They were lying back on the bed and she had no real idea how they got there. Smith's kisses had caused her to writhe helplessly in an effort to insinuate herself even closer to him and her robe had fallen away from her thighs. His hand followed the cupping of her waist to climb the throbbing softness of her small breast and his other hand slowly, deliberately untied the sash that held her robe together. When it fell apart, he gazed down on her body with a glazed look on his face. "God, but you're beautiful," he breathed. "Like a cool, untouched painting. I couldn't sleep for nights after that first day when I found you swimming in the coral pool on Chance." His lips moved over the silken skin to taste the small, rosy peak of her breast and he took her hand and moved it inside his shirt. "Touch me, darling," he growled.

The effect she had on him was electric and he moved until he was lying on top of her, resting part of his weight on his elbows to look down into her eyes. "I could so easily get lost in those sun-dappled pools . . . I can even see the reflection of vines and trees around them, did you know that?" He touched her eyebrow with a trembling fingertip and such was her trust in him that she didn't even close her eyes.

Somewhere a thousand miles away a phone rang but neither of them moved, so caught up in thralldom were they. "I've wanted to do this so many times," he told her, planting tiny kisses along the tendon of her throat. "You'll never know . . ."

"Then why didn't you?" She reached up and traced the line of his brows, those dark, slightly wicked bars that slashed so forcefully across his tanned forehead, and he caught her finger and

brought it to his mouth, nibbling on the exquisitely sensitive pad until she felt her breath
catching in shuddering gulps. "Cannibal!" she
laughed softly.

"Mmmm, that's just a starting place, darling.
My appetite for you is . . ." He proceeded to
demonstrate and she met him greedily, opening
to his kiss with a surrender that was absolute.
Love knew no refusals and this was love, of that
she was never more sure.

He stiffened a split second before they heard
someone call his name and then her door was
thrown open. "Leah, have you seen . . ."

In a sigh of infinite weariness, Smith simply
lowered his head to Leah's shoulder. "All right,
Helen, whatever it is can wait a minute. Get out
now, will you?"

The only answer was a resounding slam and
the sound of staccato steps on the stairs.

"I'm sorry, my dear," he murmured, sitting up
to rub a hand through his thick, tumbled hair.
"Helen has an unfortunate way of interrupting
at the wrong times." He reached out and pulled
the edges of her robe together and Leah, overcome by warring emotions, jerked the silky
fabric from his fingers and turned her back to
him.

"Or the right times," she snapped, struggling hard to master the desire to weep. Tears
wouldn't help anything at this point, and besides, she should be laughing, not crying. Lord
knows, it would have been infinitely harder to
leave after having been made love to by Smith
and leave she must; her very survival de-

pended on it! Besides, this cozy little threesome was growing increasingly traumatic.

Smith stood beside the bed and tucked his shirttail in. "Are you all right?"

"Of course I'm all right," she replied too brightly. "Why shouldn't I be all right?"

"Then why won't you look at me?" he asked softly.

"I think if you don't mind, I've seen altogether too much of you as it is."

"Leah, don't be like this. You know it wasn't my fault we were interrupted so why act as if I had deliberately done something to rile you . . . or hurt you."

She seethed. Her body, her mind and her heart all storming inside her for expression, she could only yell at him, "Will you just get out of my room? If I want to be 'like this,' as you call it, it's nobody's business but my own, so leave me alone, Smith Cairington . . . from now on!"

The door closed behind him with an expressive firmness before Leah was even aware of his having crossed the room. Only then did she give in to the awful aching in her throat. When Mrs. Alden tapped on her door some time later and asked if she'd like any help in getting ready for bed she said she was already almost asleep and would see her in the morning.

It was with a feeling of quiet triumph that she let herself back into the house the following afternoon. She had missed seeing both Smith and Helen by merest luck, timing her own breakfast carefully and returning to her room just as she heard Smith's office door open. He usually went downtown each morning and this she had counted on. Today, Helen was to accompany him as far as the shopping district, according to Mrs. Alden, who fussed over her as she poured the tea.

"I thought to myself last night you must be coming down with something, Miss Leah. You sounded real watery. Here, have some of these hot scones."

She'd miss the pampering, she thought now as she quietly climbed the stairs to her room. Mrs. Alden was a banty hen of a woman who simply had to mother someone and her instinct was obviously frustrated since Smith was no longer a candidate. All the help had proved to be friendly, the two dailies, the massive woman who reigned supreme in the kitchen, and the gardener who delighted her by presenting her with fresh flowers for her room each morning.

Her luck had been incredible, an omen for the future she told herself hopefully. The school had actually readied an ad for the Melbourne *Times* to appear the next day. While Leah's qualifications were not up to what they wanted, nor was her experience all that extensive, they had considered her mainly because she was experienced in areas they were just now beginning to expand and had allowed her a tour of the school. She mingled with the children, some of whom were day students and some who lived on the grounds, knowing full well she was observed.

When a boy of perhaps fourteen, grinning and dancing about her delightedly had repeatedly pounded his chest and cried, "Me Bucky, me Bucky!" she had instinctively responded by thumping her own chest and replying, "Me Leah, me Leah!"

It had been that that had tipped the scales, she was later told, her simple acceptance of his enthusiastic hug. She had neither been repulsed nor had she overreacted and within fifteen minutes, she was seated in the director's office hearing the terms of her employment.

There were a limited number of openings for cottage parents and these were already filled. However she found it possible to move into one of the larger cottages in a closet sized room as an assistant to the couple who looked after the eight children there. Leah could not believe her luck and the director, Ruth Saylor, who was well aware that the government stipend was not precisely generous, was equally pleased, despite Leah's lack of references. She had given them her stepmother's name, telling them frankly that she was only recently out from the States, and they assured her that they accepted her word for the rest.

"We don't get many layabouts looking for an easy berth here, Miss Deerfield. Anyone who actively seeks employment with our children has something special to offer; we've invariably found that to be the case."

Back in her room at Cairington Place, she began putting her things back into her bags. She had arranged for the taxi to pick her up after dinner, thus sparing her cottage mother an extra mouth on this first night. That should give her ample time to speak to Smith.

All the way home she had been quietly rehearsing her speech. There was no real reason she should tell him why she was leaving. The plain truth was evident; she couldn't be a parasite forever. It was no longer even a symbiotic relationship, for she did nothing in this well-oiled household to smooth the way. Mrs. Alden fussed over the fact that Leah tended her own room.

Standing in the open window of her room, she looked out over the garden. Even this late, bees droned lethargically on the heavy sweetness of the air, and for some reason, her throat pained her suddenly. She blinked and turned away, facing the fact that her real reason for leaving had nothing to do with independence, self-sufficiency or any of those trumped up excuses. The *real* truth was she was heart deep in love with Smith Cairington and it was pure torture to live here in his house with Helen Craddock taking her place as a long-standing part of his life. Whether they married in the near future or not, she couldn't live on the fringes, taking whatever attention he cared to spare her. If Helen had her way, she'd soon be Mrs. Cairington and even Smith admitted that whatever Helen wanted, she usually managed to get.

So . . . she'd thank him for all he'd done for her, wish him the best of everything and say goodbye. She might mention having found work but there was no real reason to tell him where.

Let him think she was leaving town, going back to Brisbane and Katherine.

By the time she had reached the door to his office, where he could usually be found at this hour, she had braced herself well and with a hand raised to rap on the door, she heard her name spoken from inside in an unfamiliar voice.

"Leah Deerfield! The New York thing? Good heaven, Smith, that makes it even worse! I'll not have this house shamed by bringing your playmates here in such a blatant manner! It's bad enough that you have Helen here so often, but of course, that's different. I mean, under the circumstances, people can't talk too much, but this . . . this little nobody you picked up in a pub somewhere! Smith, why don't you quit being so hard headed and settle down? Then there'd be no need for . . . for this sort of thing." The speaker, and it was a woman, left no doubt in anyone's mind what "this sort of thing" was and Leah cringed, one hand flying to cover her mouth as mortification covered her like a suffocating shroud.

"You'll be delighted to hear, my dear mother, that I'm planning to do just that. Quite soon now, as a matter of fact, so you can climb down out of your boughs and come greet your daughter-in-law to be."

Leah didn't wait to hear more. With a blinded look in her eyes, she ran lightly back up the stairs and shut herself in her room, one fist pushing against her mouth in an effort to hold back the sobs. She took several deep breaths, willing calmness; after all, it was not the first time she had heard words that had sent her moving on to the next place, but for some reason, rejection this time was agonizingly difficult to take. It was not only that this time . . . *this* time, it was so terribly important to walk out with her head high, to take her leave unasked. It was more than that; her heart only knew what was involved this time, for her head dared not delve too deeply.

Leaving the three packed bags, she took only her flight bag and her purse and let herself quietly out the garden door. The others were having their predinner drinks, from the sounds, and she knew she was reasonably safe from notice as she made her way around to the front of the house and started down the long driveway. Even from there, it was quite a hike to the nearest stop, but she walked mindlessly, the bag swinging unnoticed against her leg in a way that would leave bruises to be discovered later. For now, she only knew she had to get away, clean away from everything that would remind her of Smith Cairington, and she almost wished she had not lined up this job. If it weren't just such an ideal position, one that would allow her to feel needed, she'd put out her thumb and keep going in whatever direction offered first.

Leah had been at Kincaid for almost a week when she first saw something that brought her up short. She was relaxing on her one and only chair, her feet propped up on her stacked luggage, reading the papers when she came across a notice that Helen Craddock had sailed for London after a celebration involving half Melbourne's citizens, and even in an egalitarian society, Leah thought she knew *which* half.

The pain struck without warning, bringing back instant recall of the circumstances of her leaving Cairington Place, and then her more rational side took over again and she wondered why Helen was leaving. Hadn't Smith told his mother that they were to be married soon? But then, it was only natural that Helen should want to be married from her parents' home and that was in London. Smith, no doubt, would fly out later on.

The newspaper fell to the floor and she slumped in her chair, twisting her head against the lump of her ponytail. She was suddenly as tired as if she had been clenching her muscles for a week, and she supposed she had; bracing herself for the inevitable first reminder. Melbourne was a very large city and one might reasonably hope to avoid any reminder of one particular man, but when that man was a member of one of the state's most prominent families, then the odds were cut alarmingly.

She went through the motions the following week and it was only due to the enthusiasm of the children for a project she had involved them in that none of them seemed aware of her apathy. She fought against it, for she owed the children the very best she had to give but it was an uphill battle to forget the permanent ache in her heart and go on as if nothing mattered except the Kincaid Games, a sort of Olympics for the handicapped.

The children were training within their various capabilities for a contest with another school and Leah had found, by dint of much innovation, an area where almost all could compete. Those who were not actual competitors were involved in related activities and so the whole school was caught up in the scheduled affair. The idea should have brought her infinite pride, for she was a brand new, bottom of the totem pole employee and yet they had accepted her plan and rallied behind her as if she were a valued member of the staff.

She was in the pool, working with the swimming team while another group nearby worked on their broadjumps when the director entered with a small group of visitors in tow. Leah stood back to allow her pupils to do their thing, knowing they needed to become accustomed to performing before an audience before the great day. She could hear Mrs. Saylor explaining to the visitors what was going on and she felt a surge of pride. She was needed here, after all. She was making a place for herself, counting for something and it was a good feeling, a very good feeling, indeed.

An hour later, when she left the pool and went to her room to change, she received a message that the director would like to see her in her office. She showered and changed quickly into a fresh pink top and a denim skirt, then hurried along, hoping against hope that nothing was amiss. Some of the parents had taken a bit of convincing that the games would be a good thing for the children.

Ruth Saylor greeted her and then introduced her to several of the people who had visited the gym with her earlier. They were members of the board of directors and Leah smiled and shook the various hands, accepting their comments, favorable on the whole, for the games idea. When she came to an older woman, a Mrs. Hammond, however, she felt slightly uncomfortable under unusually intense scrutiny.

"And are you planning to make a career of this sort of work, Miss Deerfield?" Mrs. Hammond inquired. Her voice seemed somehow familiar but Leah could not place her. Surely she would have remembered meeting her, for the woman exuded an air of authority and quiet breeding that was attractive, if a little off-putting.

"I hope to, Mrs. Hammond," she replied.

"You're from the States, I understand. Did you have a background in this sort of work there?"

Leah supposed it was the privilege of the members of the board to ask what questions they liked of new employees and she answered to the best of her ability. There was certainly nothing offensive about the questioning and she told herself she was being silly for the slight misgiving she felt.

"It sounds as if you might find Miss Deerfield

quite irreplaceable, Mrs. Saylor," Mrs. Hammond concluded after perhaps five minutes.

While the director was assuring her that this was indeed the case, Leah was wondering at the peculiar phraseology. Was there a question of replacing her, then?

Suddenly, her secure little niche didn't seem quite so secure anymore.

Chapter Nine

The day of the games dawned clear and cool and Leah was awake even before the predawn clamor of birds outside her window. She had thrown herself wholeheartedly into the project, not only as a means of keeping her mind off Smith Cairington, either, she acknowledged with a permissible degree of self-respect.

It had taken all her persuasive powers in the beginning to convince the administration that the games not only could, but should be attempted and then, once permission was granted, it had taken even more effort to see that the children, in their awkward eagerness, did not injure themselves. She had spent a good deal of time

with an informal committee consisting of the
Physiotherapy head, Ricky Downs, and the
Occupational Therapy girl, a dynamic, chubby
redhead named Sally Sealy, to her everlasting
chagrin. Among them they had come up with
the necessary means of insuring the safety of
their charges and then the fun had begun in
earnest.

The modest arena was filled almost an hour
before the games were to start, with friends and
parents of the children of both schools and,
although the idea was certainly not a new one, it
was a first for Kincaid and its opponent, bringing
out a few representatives of the press in search
of human interest stories.

Leah had refused to take her place in the
space reserved for administration and visiting
dignitaries although, to her quiet satisfaction,
she had been invited to do so, as what Ricky
called the ringleader. Instead, she stayed with
her charges, encouraging, calming fragile
nerves and occasionally interpreting when excitement rendered a child less coherent than
usual.

Her own nerves were no problem, for now that
the moment had arrived she had relaxed the
tension that had held her together for the weeks
of preparation and she suddenly felt as if she
might sleep for a week after today. She had even
lost weight. Not only did she fill each minute of
every day, but at night, when her stiff vigilance
was relaxed, she found herself unable to keep
her mind from reaching back to Chance Island,
back to Cairington Place and the man who was

all too indelibly etched on her consciousness. That she loved him she had long since accepted: that she would probably never see him again was harder to accept, but by now, the most persistent problem she faced was making his image remain in the back of her mind instead of drifting up to haunt her at the most unexpected and inappropriate times. Being with the children made her pain easier to bear but sometimes at night when her defenses were at their lowest, she could only stare into the darkness and wonder how long before she became hardened to the nagging hurt.

By the end of the afternoon, she was both physically and emotionally at the end of her strength. The schools had been evenly rated and the wins more or less divided, but she was thrilled to see that her own Kincaid swimming team had won top honors. The children were being fêted by friends and family now and Leah flopped down on a bench in the empty gym and wiped a tendril of hair from her forehead. She had been pulled at, splashed on and even wept on more than once during the event and she looked down at her crumpled cotton dress with a rueful smile. She had dressed a bit more formally today at the veiled suggestion of the director, and a fat lot of good it had done her. She looked far more bedraggled than if she had worn her tough jeans.

The swinging door at the other end of the vast room opened to admit the Physiotherapy head. "Hello, Yank, you're tucked away here like a joey in a pouch. Been sent to hustle you up for the *giornalista.*" Ricky had spent a summer in Italy and had never got over it. He came over and dropped down beside her now, a sympathetic look in his warm, brown eyes. "Have you considered what it's going to be like tomorrow, *caro*? Big let down and all that? What do you bet we have our hands full for the next week or so until another scheme takes root in that fertile little brain of yours?"

"Whoa! I haven't thought past a shower and a twenty-four hour nap . . . haven't had time. Did you happen to see an opened box lying around marked, Pandora?"

Ricky draped an arm over her shoulders and pulled her to him in an enthusiastic hug. "You'll do, mate, you'll do. Come along now and have your picture taken with the powers that be."

"Oh, Rick, no!" she wailed.

"Oh, Rick, yes! Come on now, you're not vain, are you? I see Peggy's got your hair ribbon again. That kid's filched every ribbon that's been worn on the premises for the past three years. May as well settle for string and be done with it. She won't touch string." He tugged a hank of her long, wavy hair and pretended to lift her from the bench with it as she got wearily to her feet.

"If that's what it takes before I can hit the hay, then lead on, MacBeth," she groaned, following him out into the still brilliant sunshine.

"I think that's 'lay on, MacDuff,' but then who expects brains with all that pulchritude?"

"Who needs pulchritude, *or* brains? I'd settle for a dry pair of shoes!"

The visiting dignitaries were gathered around a table on the grounds nibbling wafer thin sandwiches and sipping tea. Leah felt dreadfully out of place among the carefully coiffed ladies in their designer casuals and pearls. They were of an age when pearls were suitable with anything. She steeled herself to follow Ricky's lead and kept her eyes carefully averted from the group until she could no longer ignore them.

"Ah, there you are, my dear. You disappeared so quickly I didn't have time to tell you that you were invited to take tea with us," Mrs. Saylor told her.

"I appreciate it, Mrs. Saylor, but as you see, I'm not fit for anything much except a strategic retreat at the moment."

"Come now, dear, don't be modest. I want you to meet these nice people and there's a reporter here who'd like to have a word with you after awhile. Mrs. Hammond, of course, you've already met, and this is Mrs. Evanston, Mr. Moreley and Dr. and Mrs. Schaeffer," the pleasant voice continued, and Leah smiled and shook the proffered hands, responding automatically to the congratulations for her part in the events of the day.

They reached the other side of the long table and she raised her eyes to see the last man she ever expected to see.

"And this is Mr. Cairington, Mrs. Hammond's son, Leah. Miss Deerfield, Mr. Cairington. Miss Deerfield, as you no doubt know, is largely responsible for today's events."

She could have said Miss Deerfield is largely

responsible for the eruption of Mount Helena for all Leah heard. She was impaled on a pair of gray eyes that were like shards of ice. No, not ice, but something burning . . . molten steel!

"Miss Deerfield and I have had the pleasure, Mrs. Saylor."

Leah could say nothing. She simply stared, dimly aware of how unfairly magnificent Smith looked in a pale gray three piece suit, an even paler gray silk shirt and a waistcoat that fit him like a glove, hinting at the sheathed muscles beneath. Was this the same man who had carried her piggyback across the island in the dark, who had slept with her cradled in his arms and placed her own trembling hands on that warm, solid body of his?

"Leah, how are you?" he asked as if none of these things had ever happened.

"I'm fine," she managed just as coolly, breaking away from his hypnotic eyes. "And you?"

"As you see me." He took her arm and led her slightly away from the others. "Shall we walk for a minute?"

"Uh . . . Smith . . . Mr. Cairington, I'd really rather go to my room now, if you don't mind. It . . . it was nice seeing you again today, but . . ."

"Leah!" The word cracked along her nerves with the shock of a bullwhip and she flinched.

"Leah," he continued in a softer, but not much softer, tone. "I think you at least owe me an explanation. What you did was unforgivable, you know."

"Yes, I suppose it was," she admitted, following his lead reluctantly. Not that she had much choice in the matter, for his hand under her elbow was not a force to be argued with. "How have you been? Oh, I asked you that, didn't I?" She was watching the progress of their feet along the path, absently aware of the difference between his sharply creased pants and gleaming bench made shoes and her own bare, tanned legs and wet sandals.

Smith remained silent until they were on the other side of a luxuriant ilex hedge and then he urged her toward a concrete bench, sitting beside her with a purposeful air. "Now, suppose we start with the reason why you ran away without even having the grace to say goodbye, not to mention, thank you for your hospitality, Mr. Cairington."

For just a second she was tempted to tell him the truth, that she had overheard his conversation with his mother and she was only anticipating being asked to move on to save herself the indignity. "I saw the school van and it occurred to me that I might find work there . . . and I did."

"Just like that?"

"Well, why not? There was certainly no reason to wait, was there? Just because you'd been stuck with me all that time was no reason for me to expect you to go on supporting me. At least on Chance I could do something to earn my keep, but there, at your house, I mean, there was nothing I could do." Her voice rose a little wildly and she made a concerted effort to get a hold of herself. She had made the break successfully and now the only thing to do was convince Smith that he need worry about her no longer, if indeed, he ever had.

"You were my guest," he continued calmly. "As that, you owed me a certain amount of consideration. Do you know that the first thing I knew of your disappearance was when Mrs. Alden told me there was a cab waiting to pick up your bags?"

"I'm sorry," she mumbled, hanging her head.

"Look at me!" he ordered peremptorially. Not waiting for her to obey the command, he took her chin in his fingers and twisted her head so that he could rake her unmercifully with those burning eyes. "I suppose I should have expected something of that nature from you, but I had forgotten what a devious little thing you could be. To have the cab deliver your bags to the bus station! You expected me to question the man, didn't you?"

Miserably, she could only nod her head. "It wasn't only that, though," she admitted in a low voice. "It was . . . well, I hated to turn up on the doorsteps here with all my worldly possessions only an hour or so after I'd gotten the job. I mean, they had only taken me on and it might look as if . . . as if . . ."

He studied her face intently, but if he drew any conclusions from the shadows beneath her clouded eyes or the tired droop of her mouth, he didn't reveal them. "You might at least have let me help you if you weren't happy at my home," he said finally, his expression unfathomable.

"But you'd helped me far too much already," she exclaimed impatiently. "Don't you see, if I was ever going to be able to stand on my own two feet, I had to make the break. When I saw that van it was like an omen . . . I knew I had to try it and it worked, so there was nothing to keep me from going. Please understand, Smith. You were under no obligation to be . . . to be as nice to me as you were and there was no way I could ever possibly begin to repay you, so . . ."

"Nice! Is that what you think? My God, Leah, I would have thought . . ." he broke off, dropping his head to his fists. His thighs were spread, his elbows resting on them and Leah could see the bunched muscles on his shoulders under the fine worsted. The subdued tie had already been loosened and Leah had an almost uncontrollable urge to unbutton the waistcoat and then the shirt and find the man who had lived with her for three weeks on a sun drenched island.

"I read that Helen had gone back to London," she said, forcing herself to bring up the name.

"That's right," he said dully.

"Will you be joining her?" she asked politely.

This time he raised his head to give her a curious, measuring look. "I might be. Why? Would you like a ride home?"

She jumped to her feet. "I don't need to hitch a ride anywhere with you . . . ever again, thank you! It's been nice seeing you again, but now I simply must run. The children . . . Mrs. Saylor . . ." she broke off on a thin, uncertain note and turned away and when she heard his

steps following her she broke into a run, covering the distance between the garden and the
side entrance to her cottage easily. She heard
him call her but she kept going. Nothing he
could say to her could help now, and she'd be
better off not even listening, not hoping anymore.

Several hours later when she had returned to
her room once more after helping to settle the
children, she was free to acknowledge to herself
the tiny germ of disappointment that Smith had
given up so easily. She indulged herself in a
series of daydreams, beginning with a Leah
dressed in her finest, mingling with the guests
over tea and greeting Smith with a poised
smile. He would melt at her unattainable love-
liness. From there, she ran the gamut, end-
ing with a continuation of the morning when
she had awakened in his arms in her bedroom
on the island. What would have happened if
Helen had not arrived when she did? Would he
have made love to her? If he had, would it have
made a difference in their relative positions
now? In this day and age, not every man felt
compelled to marry a girl under those circumstances.

Laying out her clothes for the coming day,
Leah made a conscious effort to dismiss the
childish longings from her mind. She was no
longer a shallow adolescent. She was Leah
Deerfield, daughter of a man who had turned
out to be not honorable enough, but she was
making a small contribution of her own now and

had earned a place in the lives of some very dear people. What else could she want?

Three nights later, she went to the movies with Ricky. He had taken her out before, mostly for snack suppers and a movie and once to a dance at the local hospital where he had trained. She dressed with care, for Ricky was really a very likable young man. Likable, but never lovable, at least not where she was concerned. Still, he insisted on paying for her and she knew his salary was not all that great, and so she showed her appreciation by dressing with great care for their occasional dates.

They dined on Italian food, Ricky's favorite, and saw a picture that had altogether too much noise and violence in it to suit her, although it was billed as a comedy, and when they strolled home in the cool, fragrant night air, she allowed her hand to remain in his.

He walked with her to the cottage where she stayed and they stood talking under the trellised bougainvillea that sheltered the porch for several minutes. Leah knew quite well that he was gathering his nerve to kiss her good-night and she made up her mind to let him, but when his face neared hers, she turned so that his lips raked her cheek, instead.

"Can't shoot a man for trying," he said ruefully, squeezing her hand and strolling off across campus to his own room.

She looked after him for a moment, scarcely aware of the sigh that left her lips and it was as she turned to go that she saw the tiny glowing arc beneath the sprawling shade tree at the end of the porch.

"Very touching," Smith said sarcastically, stepping out into the light.

"Smith!" she breathed softly, leaning back weakly against the stone wall that still held the heat of the day's sun.

"Leah!" he replied mockingly. He was beside her then without having seemed to move and she was aware as never before of his height, of the strength that emanated from his personality alone.

"What are you doing here?" she asked.

"Waiting for you, what did you think?"

"I didn't have any idea you were coming, or . . ."

"Or you'd have put your boy friend off? If I'd called first and asked to see you you would have taken off and not stopped running until you reached Sydney Cove."

"That's not fair. I've never run from you!"

His expression was eloquent.

"Well . . . only once, then, but what is it? Why did you need to see me?"

"Do friends have to have a reason for seeing each other then?"

"I don't know. Sometimes," she temporized. She was conscious of the difference in the fragrance of the May night . . . a mossy, spicy difference that tightened the muscles in her stomach. "But did you? Have a reason, that is?"

"Is there somewhere we can talk? I don't fancy hanging around your door like some love-sick swain . . . not like your little playmate. He comes up somewhat lacking in the romantic department, doesn't he?"

"I don't know what you mean!" she replied indignantly.

"Oh no? This is me, remember? Smith! I know you better than that!"

"I think you'd better leave now," she ground out. The last thing she needed right now was his hateful mockery!

He took her by the arm and more or less dragged her to the path and on to the parking lot, where he forced her inside his Jensen.

She could have escaped, she knew, before he reached the other door, but she didn't want to. There was an excitement in the air, some strange tension that drew her nerves to an unbearable pitch and she didn't want it to end. To her everlasting shame, she wanted to build it into such an explosive charge that it would explode and put her out of her misery.

He didn't move to start the engine; instead, he turned to face her in the dark intimacy of the car. "I did my best to stay away, you know. I'm not normally a masochist and you didn't bother to hide the fact that you have no use for my friendship."

Her heart jumped. "I . . . you . . . I didn't really mean to give you that impression," she stammered.

"Oh? Why, have you just discovered that I can be of further service to you? You need a ride somewhere, or perhaps you'd like to borrow a vacation home? Chance is occupied but I may be able to secure the *Sunfisher* for you."

"Smith, stop it! Don't be so hateful to me!" she cried. "I don't deserve that."

"Don't you? That's a matter of opinion."

Without answering she fumbled with the door latch and when it locked beneath her hand, he grabbed her, pulling her roughly away from the door. "Not yet!" he seethed. "You haven't paid me back for room, board, and traveling expenses, you know. Not since we left the island, at least."

"What?" Leah asked unbelievingly, struggling to break away from his hurtful grip. "All right! I've had a payday just last week and I'll pay whatever you say, only you'll have to take it in installments."

"Won't stretch, hmmm? Then I'll just have to come up with some other way for you to repay me, won't I?"

She didn't like his tone of voice, nor the tightening grip of his hands and she tugged away, sensing something under the surface of his control that threatened her.

With no warning, she was catapulted into his arms, hard against his chest and his hand in her hair was forcing her head backward, making her easy prey to his marauding mouth. She resisted at first, her teeth clamped tightly shut and her arms held rigid at her sides, but when he shook her again, demanding her response, she buckled like overheated metal.

"Open your mouth, you stubborn little mule," he growled against her lips, and she obeyed, offering up whatever he wanted to take from her. She was helpless against the man, as helpless as she had been that very first kiss, and she could only hope he would leave her her pride, at least, and not rob her of everything.

Why do I have to be so ridiculously vulnerable where you're concerned? What *is* there about you? She was not sure if the words were spoken aloud or merely an echo of an old refrain in her head.

Her arms found their way to his shoulders and she felt the powerful muscles moving under his warm skin as his own arms moved, one to pull her across his lap and the other to open the jacket she wore. The suit pulled aside, he went to work on her blouse and she could only utter a half-hearted protest, which he ignored completely.

"This was easier on Chance," he muttered, finding her bare flesh and stroking as if to gentle her. His hand conquered the mount of her breast, using its exquisite sensitivity against her and she responded by curling herself against him.

"Ah-h-hh, Smith, why did you have to come back into my life? I was doing so well without you . . . until I saw you again."

"Were you? You didn't look to me as if you were sleeping too well when I saw you on Sunday. Mother said you've lost weight just since she first saw you here. Could it possibly be that you're not as happy as you pretend?"

"Your mother. How was I to know who she was? If I'd known, I'd never have gone within a country mile of her, you can bet on it."

"Why?" he asked, planting featherlike little

kisses on her nose, her eyelids. "What on earth have you got against my mother?"

"No more than she has against me," Leah replied bitterly.

He was still, then, in a curiously quiet voice; "What are you talking about specifically?"

"Oh, it doesn't matter now, Smith. Leave it alone," she said wearily.

"I was afraid there might be something, but I couldn't be sure. Tell me!" His hands bit into her shoulders and she winced. Even in the dim interior, he saw, for he drew her against his chest and stroked the places where bruises would appear tomorrow. "Tell me, precious, please."

"Oh, it's just that . . . well, I heard her. That day after Helen went to have her hair done and I saw the van and . . . well, anyway, when I came downstairs the next day to tell you I had a job I heard you talking in the library."

"What did you hear? Please, Leah, it's important to me to know. You must be aware that my mother admires you tremendously now."

"Well, she certainly didn't then! I was, 'that little nobody, that Deerfield girl . . .'" Her voice broke off and he strained her to him, rocking her as he would a child who had been hurt.

"Oh, my precious, if you'd only waited to hear it all . . . or better yet, if you'd had the courage to come in and confront us."

"Not on your life! At least I've got sense enough now to get out before someone has to hit me over the head. I cut it a little fine on this one, but you've spoiled me, Smith, on Chance. I let my guard down and you sneaked in and landed one on me when I wasn't looking." She tried to laugh but it was not notably successful.

"You stupid, silly child! Hush up and listen to me a minute. No, don't move! I'm not about to let you out of my arms in the near future, so you may as well relax," he told her in no uncertain terms.

She gave in with good grace. After all, it was not as if there was anywhere else in the world she'd rather be.

"The first thing I did after we got home was to send word to Mother to drop everything and come on down to Melbourne. What I hadn't counted on was Helen's highhanded interference and that, combined with Eve's . . . well, there hadn't been time at Rockhampton to set Eve and Howard straight and when Helen barged in on us that morning . . . the second time," he added with a wry note . . . "it was to tell me that Eve was on the private line. Needless to say, by the time I got downstairs and took over, the two of them had got their heads together and got all the wrong answers. Then, Helen got on to my mother and she came running with fire in her eye to save her male child from the predatory female who had him in her clutches."

In spite of the shaft of pain that struck through her at his family's poor opinion of her, understandable though it was, Leah couldn't suppress a low gurgle and Smith joined her with a chuckle of his own.

"Yeah, well, after fending off Helen all these

many years, I'm well equipped to handle myself in that department, and well Mother knew it. All the same, she realized something was up and she left Tom—Mother married the manager of Callagong three years ago—and came hotfooting it down here to set matters straight."

"And she knows . . . about Daddy and everything."

"She'd heard of your father, Leah. He was a highly respected man for most of his life and it was obvious to anyone with half a mind that he didn't carry the weight of his . . . aberration lightly. That was probably what brought on his attack. At any rate, Mother's not concerned with what happened back in the States. She knows all the facts about how we met, about why you were over here, but it was a pure stroke of luck that she located you at Kincaid. I'd had a detective on your tail, did you know that?"

"Smith, you didn't!" she gasped, sitting up stiffly.

"You're darn right I did, and let me tell you something, my little darling, you reduced the very best of them to a mass of humiliation. The very simplicity of what you did stumped them, I guess. But then, who'd look for a slip of a girl with no money, no experience, and no known friends at a place like this? Anyway, when Mother told me after I returned from Brisbane and Rockhampton, where I'd gone to search in person, that she'd located a Leah Deerfield at Kincaid, I was fit to be hogtied!"

"But you didn't try to get in touch with me."

"Yes, and I practically had to nail myself to the wall to keep from it, but then, you hadn't left me with much reason to think you'd welcome a visit from me. Besides, if I'd confronted you at a place where you could get away from me, I was pretty certain you'd do just that . . . and you did, didn't you? In spite of all my clever plans."

"I . . . oh, Smith, I didn't know it meant anything to you, to see me again, that is," she offered so softly that he had to lean closer to catch her words.

"Didn't know! Good heavens, woman, what do I have to do to let you know what it means to me . . . what *you* mean to me?"

Startled, she recoiled. "Well, you might try telling me."

"When have I had the chance?" he demanded with a heavy sigh.

"Who's stopping you now?"

"When it comes to blurting it out, I'm not at all sure I know how," he told her wryly. "Leah Deerfield, I love you. I've never even come close to saying that to a woman before . . . or feeling it."

"Oh, Smith, if only I'd known," she whispered feelingly.

"Well, why else would I have brought you home with me? I could have dropped you off anywhere along the way! Why did you think I wouldn't risk letting you out of my sight?"

"An overdeveloped social conscience, maybe? Anyway, you *did* let me out of your sight . . . I know, I know, it was business and Mrs. Alden told me you had let things slip while you were gone. But Smith, there was Helen, and what was I to think? It was pretty obvious that the two of you were awfully close. Why else would she join you at Chance? And besides, she said . . ."

"Forget Helen and what she might have said. I grew up with that conniving female and for the past ten years or so, ever since she took it in her head that it might be fun to be Mrs. Cairington Enterprises, she's probed every sign of weakness and struck like lightning. I've had the devil's own time staying one jump ahead of her, but I honestly believe it was more for the sport of the chase than any real desire for the prize . . . if you call me a prize."

"I call you a prize," Leah said firmly, tracing his eyebrows with a slightly unsteady finger. "I call you everything any woman could possibly want in a man. I call you more than a little bit conceited, more arrogant by half than most, and I call you . . ."

"You had better call me yours, because I am, you know. Try getting away from me now and I'll carry you back to Chance and scuttle the boat! Come here, you disrespectful little wretch, and let me show you what's in store for you for the next half century or so," he growled, and proceeded to demonstrate.

When she could breathe again, she pulled away from him slightly. "Smith," she said hesitantly, "I can't leave the school completely."

"Hmm, no, maybe not. But then the Cairington women have always been involved in something or other of that nature, so suppose we let you work on a volunteer basis say, one day a week."

"Make it three," she countered.

"One!"

"Two?"

"Done. That's after the honeymoon, of course. Not even your precious swimming team could expect you to commute from Chance."

"Hmmm, a honeymoon on Chance," she murmured, nuzzling the warm spot under his ear until he caught his breath with a muffled groan.

"Honey, you're going to have to resign yourself to the fact that we're going to have the shortest engagement in history. The next time I get you in a bed, I'm barring the door, and that time won't be long in coming." He pulled her back across his lap and made no attempt to disguise the state of his desire for her. "I'll call Eve and tell her to hit the trail again, hmmm?"

"Will she mind?" Leah asked doubtfully. "We could always go somewhere else."

"She'll be delighted. It'll mean she's seen the last of Helen and that will suit the whole family. Helen, in case you haven't guessed, was the package I took reluctant delivery of. I knew she was headed my way and it seemed polite to remove myself from the scene until she got tired of hanging around and went back home to Papa, who, incidentally, was one of my Dad's closest friends."

"Won't he be upset at your . . . well, at Helen and you . . ."

"He's got better sense than that. Helen needs some meek mannered fellow she can put on a leash, and . . ."

"And they don't make a leash strong enough to fit you," Leah gurgled.

Sometime later, Smith whispered into her ear, "I'm going to make love to you in all the places where you've tempted me almost beyond endurance."

"The coral pool?" she teased breathlessly.

"That'll be the first one."

"I love you, Smith. I feel as if I were a small part of an enormous picture puzzle that's finally found its notch. Does that sound crazy?"

Against the sweet perfume of her hair, he told her that, no, it didn't seem crazy at all. "The picture has a vague familiarity, too, as if I've seen it somewhere in the long distant past, and besides, considering the way we're going to fit into each other's lives and bodies, it's an apt analogy, my precious love," he murmured.

She ran her hands beneath his shirt to thread her fingers in the crisp body hair on his chest, loving the feel of him, the scent of him, and the way he made her body respond.

"I'd better get you inside quickly, you little devil, or we're going to begin fitting that particular puzzle together right now."

Silhouette **Romance**

15-Day Free Trial Offer
6 Silhouette Romances

6 Silhouette Romances, free for 15 days! We'll send you 6 new Silhouette Romances to keep for 15 days, absolutely free! If you decide not to keep them, send them back to us. We'll pay the return postage. You pay nothing.

Free Home Delivery. But if you enjoy them as much as we think you will, keep them by paying us the retail price of just $1.50 each. We'll pay all shipping and handling charges. You'll then automatically become a member of the Silhouette Book Club, and will receive 6 more new Silhouette Romances every month and a bill for $9.00. That's the same price you'd pay in the store, but you get the convenience of home delivery.

Read every book we publish. The Silhouette Book Club is the way to make sure you'll be able to receive every new romance we publish.

This offer expires July 31, 1981

READERS' COMMENTS ON SILHOUETTE ROMANCES:

"Every one was written with the utmost care. The story of each captures one's interest early in the plot and holds it all through until the end."

—P.B.,* Summersville, West Virginia

"Silhouette Books are so refreshing that they take you into different worlds. . . . They bring love, happiness and romance into my life. I hope Silhouette goes on forever."

—B.K., Mauldin, South Carolina

"What I really enjoy about your books is they happen in different parts of the U.S.A. and various parts of the world. . . ."—P.M., Tulia, Texas

"I was happy to see another romance-type book available on the market—Silhouette—and look forward to reading them all."

—E.N., Washington, D.C.

"The Silhouette Romances are done exceptionally well. They are so descriptive . . ."

—F.A., Golden, Colorado

* names available on request

Silhouette Romance

ROMANCE THE WAY IT USED TO BE...
AND COULD BE AGAIN

Contemporary romances for today's women.
Each month, six very special love stories will be yours
from SILHOUETTE. Look for them wherever books are sold
or order now from the coupon below.

$1.50 each